Surviving Jamestown

THE ADVENTURES OF YOUNG SAM COLLIER

To Joyce Henson, who embarks on so
many adventures with me.
—GLK

Published by
PEACHTREE PUBLISHERS
1700 Chattahoochee Avenue
Atlanta, Georgia 30310-2112

www.peachtree-online.com

Text © 2001 by Gail Langer Karwoski
Illustrations © 2001 by Paul Casale

Cover and book design by Loraine M. Joyner
Book composition by Melanie McMahon Ives

Manufactured in January 2010 in Bloomsburg, PA by R.R. Donnelley & Sons in the United States of America

10 9 8 7 6 5 4 3 (hardcover)
10 9 8 7 6 (trade paperback)

Library of Congress Cataloging-in-Publication Data

Karwoski, Gail, 1949–
    Surviving Jamestown : the adventures of young Sam Collier / Gail Langer Karwoski ; illustrated by Paul Casale.--1st ed.
        p. cm.
    Summary: Sam Collier, a twelve-year-old, serves as page to John Smith during the relentless hard ship experienced by the founders at the first permanent English settlement in the New World.
    ISBN 13: 978-1-56145-239-2 / ISBN 10: 1-56145-239-4 (hardcover)
    ISBN 13: 978-1-56145-245-3 / ISBN 10: 1-56145-245-9 (trade paperback)
    1. Jamestown (Va.)--Juvenile fiction. 2. Smith, John, 1580-1631.--Juvenile fiction. 3. Collier, Samuel, d. 1622.--Juvenile fiction. [1. Jamestown (Va.)--Fiction. 2. Smith, John, 1580-1631.--Fiction. 3. Collier, Samuel, d. 1622.--Fiction. 4. Explorers--Fiction. 5. Virginia--History--Colonial period, ca. 1600-1775--Fiction.] I. Casale, Paul, ill. II. Title.

PZ7.K153 Su 2001
[Fic]--dc21   00-054859

Surviving Jamestown

THE ADVENTURES OF YOUNG SAM COLLIER

Gail Langer Karwoski

Illustrated by
Paul Casale

PEACHTREE
ATLANTA

Acknowledgments

Lots of people helped me bring this story to the page. Any inaccuracies or misjudgments are mine, but I have many people to thank for contributions to this work.

My husband, Chester Karwoski, deserves my biggest thanks. Without his support and enthusiasm, I would not be a writer. His suggestions make my stories clearer and more lively.

Many experts graciously reviewed the manuscript to help ensure its accuracy. Nancy Egloff, the historian at the Jamestown Settlement, reviewed multiple drafts and researched many period details at my request. Ruth Haas, also from the Jamestown Settlement, supplied numerous helpful suggestions, as did Diane Stallings and Lee Pelham Cotton from the Colonial National Historical Park and Judith A. Corello and Christa Mueller from the Association for the Preservation of Virginia Antiquities. All have been very generous with their time and knowledge.

Dr. Stephen Lucas helped me with the medical moments in the story. Steve is an exceptional physician who cares not only for his patients, but also for his patient's characters!

I appreciate the expert advice of the PACE students of Joyce Henson and Cass Robinson at Malcom Bridge Elementary in Oconee County, Georgia, who helped me select the title for this book.

The members of my writers' "family" (the Four at Five: Bettye Stroud, Wanda Langley, and Lori Hammer) evaluated each chapter and listened sympathetically to tribulations along the way! Another Peachtree writer, Adrian Fogelin, also offered helpful suggestions. My daughters, Leslie and Geneva Karwoski, gave me my first lessons in children's literature many years ago; as grown-ups, they are still giving me valuable insights and invaluable encouragement. My parents, Farley and Charlotte Langer, are—as always—my greatest fans!

So many folks at my publishing "family," Peachtree Publishers, Ltd., have devoted time and support to this book! Associate Editor Vicky Holifield was wonderful, gentle, and brilliant in her copyediting, trimming, and proofing. Production Manager Melanie McMahon and Art Director Loraine Balcsik carefully crafted these pages and worked hard to make this a beautiful book. Most of all, I owe an enormous thanks to my editor, Sarah Helyar Smith. Sarah embraced this project. She's an awesome editor—tireless and talented—who cares deeply about producing high-quality books for young readers.

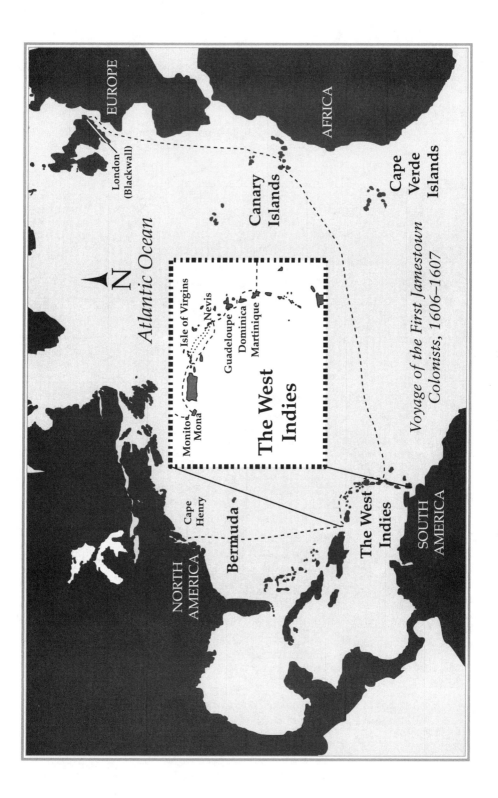

EUROPE

AFRICA

London
(Blackwall)

Canary
Islands

Cape
Verde
Islands

Atlantic Ocean

N

Isle of Virgins

Nevis

Guadeloupe

Dominica

Martinique

Monito
Mona

The West
Indies

Voyage of the First Jamestown
Colonists, 1606–1607

Cape
Henry

Bermuda

NORTH
AMERICA

The West
Indies

SOUTH
AMERICA

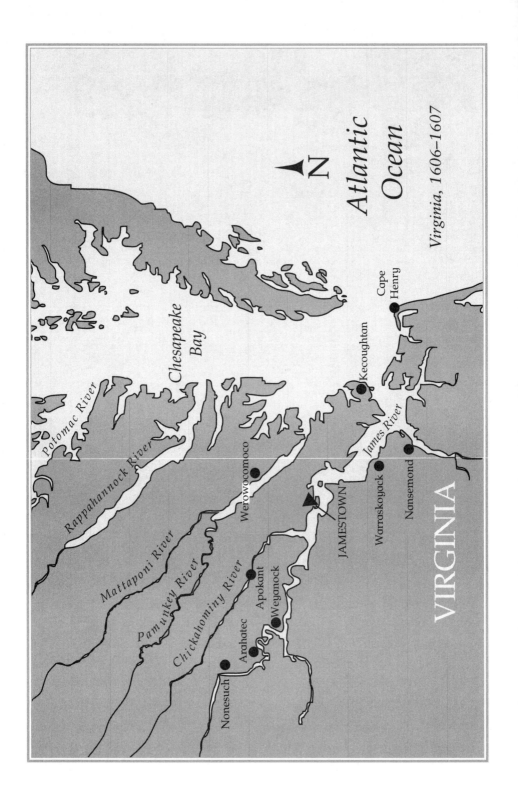

Contents

Preface

English ships explored the coast of North America for more than a century before England successfully planted a colony in the New World.

After Columbus discovered the West Indies in 1492, and all through the 1500s, ships from England, Spain, and France made many voyages to the coast of North America. Pirates sailed the American waters, too.

England made its first attempts to establish a North American colony in the 1580s. In 1584, Sir Walter Raleigh founded a colony on Roanoke Island, off the coast of what is now North Carolina. Nobody knows what happened to this "lost colony."

By the beginning of the 1600s, England, Spain, and France each claimed land in North America and tried to hold onto those claims by starting permanent settlements. In 1620, the Mayflower *set sail to found the Plymouth Colony. But fourteen years earlier, in 1606, King James I had chartered the Virginia Company of London, and its first fleet set sail in December of the same year.*

The fleet reached Chesapeake Bay in 1607. The settlement they established became Jamestown—England's first permanent North American colony.

The Luckiest Boy in England

Sam Collier climbed onto the ship's broad railing and sat with his legs dangling. He stuck two fingers in his mouth—the way his new friend Nate Peacock had taught him—and let fly a screeching whistle. Grabbing a line to steady himself, he placed his feet on the wooden railing and slowly rose until he stood, teetering, on the side of the swaying ship. Grinning, he announced, "Samuel Collier, second son of Thomas and Anne Collier of Lincolnshire, is the luckiest boy in all of England!"

There was no response from the people on the wharf at Blackwall Port. With night coming on, and the sailors busy loading supplies, none of the men on the ship paid attention to Sam's announcement, either.

But a boy's voice behind him said, "Sam Collier will be none too lucky if he falls into the black water of the Thames River!"

Startled, Sam turned around.

Nate imitated the voice of a nagging parent. "How many times do I need to remind you, Samuel? A ship makes a slippery perch." He wagged his index finger. "If you fall in wearing your heavy coat, you'll sink like a stone." He glared at Sam for a few seconds, then burst out laughing.

Smiling, Sam leaped onto the muddy deck, his feet skidding on the slick wooden boards.

"Master Smith told me to fetch you," Nate said.

Sam was John Smith's page. For the next few years, he would be expected to obey Master Smith the way a son obeys his father. As a page, Sam was Smith's servant who had to help with all kinds of errands and chores. But he was also Smith's apprentice, and he would have a chance to learn whatever his master was willing to teach. Sam knew that when a page became fifteen or sixteen years old and ready to strike out on his own, he sometimes followed in his master's footsteps. John Smith was an explorer and an adventurer, and Sam thought this life would suit him just fine.

Waving good-bye to the people on the wharf, Sam trotted after Nate. Nobody waved back, but Sam didn't notice.

The boys were a mismatched pair. Sam was twelve, nearly two years younger than Nate, and he stood at least a head shorter than his friend. Although he was lean, Sam's muscular body made him seem stocky compared with his skinny friend. Nate's long arms and legs stuck out of his coat sleeves and pants, ending in huge hands and clumsy feet. In his woolly waistcoat, Nate resembled a lanky, cheerful pup who had not yet grown bulky enough to fill up his own skin.

"Do you know any of those folks?" Nate asked, gesturing at the crowd on the wharf.

"Not a one," Sam replied. "I've never been to this port. For that matter, I'd never been on the Thames River or to the city of London until I came aboard this ship. And I don't care to return to any of these places, either."

Nate nodded in agreement. "Too crowded," he said. "I don't like seeing so many faces without a friendly look on any of them."

"I don't want to be friends with them," Sam said. "They live in the old world. If you ask me, even the great city of London is dirty and worn out. It's part of the past. You and me, we're

A boy's voice said, "Sam Collier will be none too lucky if he falls into the black water of the Thames River!"

headed for a new world—the future!" Sam clamped his hand on Nate's shoulder, and the boys looked at each other and grinned.

They threaded their way along the railing of the crowded ship. The deck of the *Susan Constant* was smaller than the ground floor of the tidy farmhouse where Sam had grown up. But the ship was crowded with seventeen sailors shouting directions and loading cargo. And more than fifty passengers were living aboard this ship.

The boys had to clamber over coils of tarred rope and heaps of equipment. They jumped aside to avoid bumping into sailors, who were carrying heavy barrels on board and passing them down to their mates for storage in the hold. Some of the gentlemen passengers stood watching the bustle. Their overcoat collars were pulled up against the damp December chill.

As they squeezed between groups of onlookers, Sam and Nate nearly bumped into a small, white-faced boy.

"Nathaniel Peacock!" the boy shouted. "I've been searching high and low for you." James Brumfield frowned. "Master Calthrop sent me to find you. He's worried sick that you got off the ship and got lost here in Blackwall. I do think you should be more considerate. We're not supposed to make trouble for the gentlemen, you know."

Nate started to hurry off, but Sam grabbed his arm and winked. "Wait a minute, Nate. I hope you paid attention to James's pretty speech."

James hesitated. He considered Sam Collier a rude boy, so the compliment surprised him. He wasn't sure whether he should tip his cap to acknowledge Sam's fair words. Or whether Sam was being sarcastic and had insulted him.

Sam looked closely at James's pale face. *It's as white as a fish belly!* Sam thought. With a quick movement, Sam snatched James's cap and tossed it to Nate. Then Sam grabbed the two ends of James's blue scarf and tied them over the boy's mouth. "It's not considerate of you to go bareheaded in this damp, chilly weather, James Brumfield," Sam said, grinning. "Look, your lips are turning blue with cold! We're not supposed to make trouble for the gentlemen, you know."

Nate held James's cap above the boy's head. When James jumped to grab it, Nate tossed the cap on top of a tall stack of crates. Chuckling, Sam and Nate ran off in search of their masters.

Sam climbed down the wooden stairs to the 'tween deck, the middle deck where the passengers would live during the voyage. He found John Smith rearranging some crates. Smith's sleeves were rolled up to his elbows, and he'd taken off his waistcoat. Beads of sweat glistened on his broad forehead and dripped onto his short, brown beard.

"Make haste, lad," Smith said as he strained to move a heavy crate. "I want to be sure none of these guns or powder boxes will get wet."

Sam pulled off his cap and stuffed it into his pocket. His wavy brown hair was plastered to his head, and he ran his fingers through it. Loosening his coat, Sam reached for the stack of guns and ammunition. "Are we taking all these guns for hunting in Virginia?" he asked.

"Mostly for defense," Smith said. We may run into pirates on the islands. Or Spanish ships."

Sam raised his eyebrows. "Do you think we'll have to fight off pirates? Or Spaniards?"

Smith shrugged. "Pirates would gladly steal our ship and all its cargo. As for the Spanish, they want to claim as much of North America as they can, so they'd be delighted to prevent us from reaching Virginia. Believe me, lad, I've met my share of dangers outside England. I know how crucial our weapons will be."

A sliver of fear slid into Sam's stomach, but he tried to ignore it. *This is my chance to see the world beyond my father's farm,* he reminded himself. Sam shifted the crates as Smith directed. Then Smith showed him how to lash them securely in place so they would not overturn when high seas rocked the ship.

"When do we set sail for Virginia, Master Smith?" Sam asked.

"Tonight, on the tide. The sailors have almost finished loading the hold. As soon as the tide shifts, our fleet will continue down the Thames. Then we set out across the Atlantic Ocean."

"Will we be in North America by Christmas?" Sam asked.

John Smith smiled. "The winds don't blow that fast, lad! It's already December 20. We'll be lucky to reach the Canary Islands—off the coast of Africa—by the beginning of the new year."

"Is it true, Master Smith, that North America is colder than England, and its winds are so fierce they can blow apart a ship in an instant?"

Before Smith had a chance to answer, Sam plunged ahead. "...and that naked men run over the land—men who have no fear of death and cannot speak any better than wolves?" Sam's eyes sparkled. "And that rivers of liquid gold flow through the countryside and shine in the rays of the sun?"

John Smith frowned. "Somebody's been filling your ears with fabulous tales! It's best not to swallow every word you're served aboard ship. When I lived among the Turks, I learned it was wiser to see a thing with my own eyes rather than believe the tales that men tell."

Smith stood and mopped sweat off his forehead. He was a short man, lean but muscular. Every inch of his small frame seemed necessary to support the man's actions, just as every word he spoke seemed to have a purpose. Smith looked at his page and continued. "There's a great deal of land across the sea,

Sam. Along the coast they call Newfoundland, they say winters are much colder than here in England. But our ships are headed south for Virginia," Smith explained. "We plan to drop anchor near Roanoke Island, not far from where Sir Walter Raleigh's ships landed. The climate is mild where we're headed."

"Have you also heard that naked men live there, Master Smith?" Sam persisted. "And that there are rivers of gold?"

Smith nodded. "Yes, Sam, I've heard the tales about naked men who live in North America. I was told these natives have mild, simple natures—as gentle as small children. If the tales are true, we can expect an easy welcome from them. And I've also heard the stories about fabulous deposits of gold." Smith rubbed his neck. "We shall see for ourselves soon enough."

Sam waited hopefully. Although he had known John Smith for only a few weeks, Sam had already discovered that when his master was in a talkative mood he could tell wonderful stories of shipwrecks and captures, of bold escapes and rich rewards. All of Smith's stories were about his own experiences in faraway places. And every word of them was true!

When John Smith was fifteen, his father had apprenticed him to a rich merchant. But he found a merchant's life too dull. So, when he turned seventeen, Smith left the merchant and went to fight in the Dutch war of independence. As soon as the war was over, Smith went to sea. His hunger for adventure still strong, he joined the Austrian army in a war against the Turks. Before long, he was in the thick of battle, beheading Turkish officers. Then he was wounded and captured. Forced into slavery, he made a daring escape and fled to Transylvania. He was rewarded handsomely for his courage and returned to England a prosperous man.

Smith looked at the crowd of passengers and sailors hurriedly stowing the last of the supplies, then turned to Sam. "If we find gold, Sam Collier, you'll return to Lincolnshire a rich man.

You'll be richer than your older brother, in spite of the farm that he'll inherit."

Sam's father was a farmer. According to custom, their oldest son, Thomas Jr., would inherit the family farm. Sam had to make his own way in the world. All his parents could offer their second son was a brief education, a stock of warm clothing and leather shoes, and a position with a man like Smith.

"I'm never going to return to Lincolnshire!" Sam replied. "I'm going to be a man of Virginia and swim in rivers of gold. I think I'm the luckiest boy in England," Sam declared, "setting out on such an adventure before my thirteenth birthday!"

Smith nodded. "Perhaps you are, Sam. I believe you're a fine lad for this journey—bold and eager. When I was your age, I was the same sort of lad."

~

The *Susan Constant*, followed by her companion ships the *Godspeed* and the *Discovery*, made her way down the Thames River and into the English Channel. One hundred and five English passengers and forty sailors rode aboard the Virginia Company's fleet. The men were hoping to find profit as well as adventure in Virginia. Their goal was to establish a colony that would send goods and raw materials back to England for sale. Sea captains had been bringing back reports of vast forests and abundant game, and England needed timber and furs. Furthermore, the Virginia Company hoped the settlers would find deposits of gold and gemstones. And if they were able to find an easy route across the Americas to the Orient, then the Virginia colony might become a trading center for China's expensive silks and spices.

But when the ships reached the Channel, the winds blew hard from the south, and the fleet was stalled in sight of the English coast. Since the ships couldn't sail into the head winds, the passengers were allowed on deck for a few hours each after-noon when the seas weren't too high.

Sam and Nate didn't mind the delay. There was so much to see on a sailing ship! When the sailors weren't busy, the boys pestered them with questions about how the *Susan Constant* worked. Most of the sailors ignored Sam and Nate, but a few of the older crew members enjoyed showing the boys how to maneuver the sails to catch the wind. Sometimes they let the boys climb on the ship's rigging to get a better view of the coast of England and the choppy waters that skidded toward shore.

When the weather turned foul, the passengers had to stay below, on the 'tween deck. With more than fifty people and all their possessions crammed into the tight space, the 'tween deck was very crowded. The hatches were closed to keep seawater from spilling in, and lanterns provided only dim light.

At night the gentlemen passengers and some of the sailors slept in hammocks hung from wooden posts. The boys and the laborers slept on straw pallets or blankets spread across the damp floorboards. The ship rocked constantly with the motion of the sea, and many passengers became seasick. The combina-tion of dampness, sweat, and vomit gave the 'tween deck a ter-rible smell. Sam was used to strong farm odors like manure, but the passenger's living area smelled much worse than the filthiest barn.

For Sam, the worst part of life aboard ship was the noise. In addition to passengers talking and sick men moaning, the wooden ship groaned and creaked. When the wind shrieked through the rigging and waves crashed against the hull, Sam had to shout to make himself heard. Even in calm weather, Sam could still hear the constant slap, slap of water against the hull.

Besides Sam and Nate, James was the only other boy aboard the *Susan Constant*. Already puny, James lost weight in those first weeks at sea. As soon as the sea grew rough, James's pale face turned greenish and he complained that he felt dizzy. When the ship rocked on big waves, James got sick. The motion of the gray, wintry waters churned up his insides and squeezed them empty of all comfort. His master, Edward Wingfield, scolded him when he fouled the sleeping quarters with his vomit.

Sometimes Sam and Nate were told to lead James on deck and hold him steady by the side of the railing. Sam dreaded that task. Whenever they went to fetch him, James pleaded with them to let him stay below. The boy's face took on a look of pure terror when he beheld the open sea. Although Sam felt ashamed for James's cowardice and thought it was disgusting to watch him throw up, Sam held the boy's arms as gently as he could. James was plainly embarrassed to seem such a weakling, but he could not force his guts to make peace with the water.

Seasickness wasn't the only ailment to trouble the passengers. Some of the men caught bad colds. The Reverend Robert Hunt developed such a terrible cough that Captain Newport wanted to take him back to England. But the minister kept refusing, saying he'd be well soon enough. One day, Hunt motioned to Sam as the boy trotted by. He told Sam to find John Smith.

Sam returned quickly with his master.

"John," rasped Hunt, "I ask your support. As a minister, I have a duty to fulfill for the Company. And I refuse—" A fit of coughing interrupted his words.

Smith pointed at a pitcher. Sam quickly filled the minister's cup with water and handed it to him.

Hunt nodded at Sam as he took the cup. He sipped, trying to regain control of his voice. At last, he handed Sam the empty cup, cleared his throat, and continued. "I won't hear of returning to England, John. More than a hundred Englishmen are aboard these ships setting out for a strange, wild shore. Who knows what dangers and hardships these men will face? As a minister, I am the shepherd of this flock. Prayer offers a mighty comfort in times of stress and danger—" Again the racking coughs cut off Hunt's words.

Without waiting to be told, Sam handed another cup of water to Hunt. The minister's eyes glowed in his pale face like two embers embedded in ash. When he coughed, his thin cheeks flushed a bright red.

Smith sat beside Hunt and waited for the coughing to stop. "You have my full support," Smith said to the clergyman. "If you choose to make the crossing, I promise no man will force you to turn back. But if you choose to return to England, no man shall criticize your decision in my presence."

"I will not turn back," Hunt declared.

Smith smiled and gently laid a hand on the minister's thin shoulder. "I'm convinced you take your orders from a higher authority, Reverend. I'll speak to our ship's captain. I give you my word that there'll be no more talk of sending you back to England."

Sam was up early the next morning, glad to see that the sky was clear. He was on deck with Smith when Nate and his master, Stephen Calthrop, joined them. Sam and Nate grinned at each other.

Calthrop greeted Smith. "I understand you spoke with Captain Newport yesterday," said Calthrop. He lowered his voice. "About Reverend Hunt's desire to remain on board."

Smith nodded. The two men edged closer together and positioned themselves downwind from the sailors so their conversation could not be heard, but Sam could still hear every word. "Yes, Reverend Hunt asked me to support him," Smith said. "He believes he has a duty to remain on board. The colonists need his spiritual guidance."

Calthrop eyed Smith carefully. "You made Captain Newport angry, John. He has told several of the gentlemen on board that you spoke too forcefully. That you're quick to command, but reluctant to listen to your betters. If I may borrow the captain's words, you 'lack the manners of a peasant, but you're as arrogant as an earl!'" Calthrop laughed. "I think it's fair to say that you left the captain as angry as a cat in a sack!"

Smith frowned. "After our meeting, the captain agreed to keep Reverend Hunt on board. The captain's mood is of no importance to me. Furthermore," Smith added stiffly, "I don't care what he thinks of my social status or my manners."

Calthrop raised his eyebrows. "Be careful, John. There are powerful men on these ships. Men who believe their opinions are law." Calthrop paused, his brow wrinkled. "If Reverend Hunt were to die during the crossing, it would cast a shadow across the Virginia Company's first venture. Some of the gentlemen might blame you for insisting that we keep such a sick man aboard ship."

"That's absurd, Stephen!" Smith sputtered. "I'm an explorer, not a doctor. And I'm not a fortuneteller, either. I sincerely hope Reverend Hunt recovers his health. But ailing or healthy, the man believes it's his duty to look after the spiritual needs of our colony. I respect Hunt, so I stood up for him. I won't beg forgiveness when I stand up for my friends."

Calthrop smiled. "Hold your temper, man. I'm just telling you what's afoot. I'm not agreeing with your critics." Calthrop put an arm on Smith's shoulder, and the two men stared out over the waves. "You know my thoughts, John. We have a new world to conquer. We need men like you—men with skill and daring. I just don't want you to anger the captain or the gentlemen."

Sam and Nate listened as their masters talked. Smith lacked Calthrop's cultured manners, Sam noticed. It was as if Smith didn't have the time to be polite. Unlike the highborn Calthrop,

Smith came from the merchant class of English society. Since he had not inherited power or wealth, he had learned to grab for any chance of success.

Nate had told Sam a lot about his master. Calthrop was only four years younger than Smith, but he was far younger in his experience of the world. His aristocratic family was related to Master Edward Wingfield, the most powerful gentleman aboard the *Susan Constant*. Calthrop was going to Virginia in search of adventure. As the third son in his family, he would never control his father's lands, so he hoped to find his own special future in the new world.

Sam and Nate leaned against the ship's rail. When it seemed like their masters would continue talking all afternoon, Sam challenged Nate to arm wrestle. Long-armed Nate, as usual, was winning the contest until Sam called out, "Look, a dolphin! Over there!"

Nate swung around, and Sam slammed down his arm.

"Hey, that's cheating!" Nate yelped.

"No, it's not," Sam said. "I was just using my brain along with my arm!"

Nate snatched Sam's cap and took off. Laughing, Sam chased after him. The two dodged between crates and ropes. Panting, they nearly collided with a sailor. Master Edward Wingfield had just climbed up to the deck when Nate slammed into him.

"Upon my word!" exclaimed Wingfield. "Watch out where you're going!"

Ignoring Wingfield, Sam caught up to Nate and jumped on him, knocking them both onto the wooden planks. Frowning, Wingfield pulled them to their feet by their collars and called to Smith and Calthrop.

"Look here!" Wingfield shouted. "These boys were running wildly on deck. They nearly knocked me down. A ship is no place for such ill-mannered behavior." Wingfield pursed his lips and pointed a finger at his cousin. "Stephen, I do not understand why you decided to bring along a servant. You are young enough to attend to your own needs without help. But if you must have these boys around, I insist you keep them under control."

Smith opened his mouth to answer, but Calthrop jumped in. "Terribly sorry, Master Edward," Calthrop said. "We will certainly have a talk with the lads about shipboard manners." Calthrop gave the boys a stern look.

Wingfield cleared his throat and stomped off.

Calthrop turned to the boys and winked. "If you boys have to bump into a gentleman, please bump into somebody besides my kinsman, Master Edward. Bump into someone with a better sense of balance. Or at least a better sense of humor!" Calthrop grinned at his own joke.

"If there's another complaint about the boys, I'll speak to Master Wingfield," Smith snapped. "I will tell him that these boys belong on this ship. We are going to build a colony in Virginia, and these boys are strong enough to work hard and young enough learn new skills. Indeed, what will a refined gentleman like Master Wingfield be able to contribute? If he cannot even keep his balance when a boy brushes past him, he will surely be of less use in the wilderness than a linen tablecloth!"

Calthrop laughed. "I do hope you don't speak such thoughts to Master Edward, John. You'll get yourself in serious trouble. Remember—he's the only member of the Virginia Company on board." Calthrop looked at the choppy waters. "We've been stalled here for almost five weeks. I think everyone is losing patience."

The Crossing

At the end of January, the winds finally changed direction, and the fleet set sail. The three ships headed south along the coast of Europe, and then they turned west to make a great arc across the Atlantic Ocean. By traveling this semicircular route, they would take advantage of the trade winds that blew across the sea to North America.

On February 17, they reached the Canary Islands, sixty miles northwest of Africa. Captain Newport ordered the small fleet to drop anchor. He wanted to send sailors ashore to collect fresh water and gather firewood for cooking during their voyage. Four or five days in the islands would also give them a chance to hunt for game that could be salted for the trip.

The *Susan Constant* carried a longboat, and this large rowboat had room for thirty men. All three of the ships also carried smaller boats so the sailors could row ashore from deeper water where the ships would anchor. When the sailors made ready to row to the beach with great wooden barrels to fill with fresh drinking water, Sam and Nate begged their masters to let them go ashore. After the gloom and chill of England's winter, the Canary Islands looked so inviting! Soft, warm breezes soothed their skin, and sparkling sands invited them to run and stretch. The boys were not the only passengers eager to refresh themselves on land. All the Englishmen were grateful when Captain Newport ordered the sailors to ferry them to the beach.

As soon as Sam and Nate climbed down into the longboat, they began to unlace their heavy leather shoes. They rolled down their stockings, stuffed them into the shoes, and were ready to leap into the surf as soon as the boat neared the beach. "Race you to the dunes!" Sam called and took off with a splash.

Nate easily passed him. His long legs leaped over the water, while Sam had to churn through the foamy waves.

"Have you spent so long aboard a ship that you've forgotten how to run, Sam Collier?" Nate teased over his shoulder.

Panting, the boys ran up the beach. Nate won, but neither boy wanted to stop running. They had been cooped up in that cramped ship for weeks! The boys dropped their shoes on the sand and headed for the green woods beyond the dunes. They spotted a climbing tree with low, thick branches. But before they could scramble up its squat trunk, they heard John Smith's voice behind them.

"Sam! Nate! Come back here!"

The boys turned and ran back to the bright strip of sand.

"Don't get out of earshot, lads," Smith warned. "You're not in England anymore. It's not safe to go running off where you can't be seen or heard. From now on, we're in danger of attack, so you need to be careful."

Just then, Master Wingfield came striding up the beach with little James scurrying along behind him. Wingfield confronted Smith. "What's this I hear about bringing the guns on shore? The sailors say you've ordered them back to the ships to get the guns."

"Yes," Smith answered, "I told them to go get some of the guns. The last time I was aboard a ship in these islands, we were attacked by pirates. I think it was unwise for us to choose this southern route across the ocean. But it was Captain Newport's decision. Now that we've reached the Canary Islands, I think it's unsafe to leave our weapons aboard ship."

Wingfield frowned. "As for your opinions about the wisdom of our route, Smith, you have voiced them several times. I did not find them compelling before, and neither did Captain Newport, who, as you know, is the admiral in command of this entire fleet. My concern now is that you overstepped your authority and gave orders to the sailors. Were you relaying a command from Captain Newport?" Wingfield demanded, his finger pointing at Smith's chest. "We can't have every passenger giving orders to the sailors. There has to be a chain of command. If you have something to say—"

"I told the sailors to get the guns, Master Wingfield," Smith interrupted, his voice rising. "I decided that we were putting ourselves in danger—"

"You decided, Mr. Smith?" Wingfield snapped. "Since when do you make these decisions?"

"Since the Lord gave me a brain to reason with. Look here—"

"No, you look here!" shouted Wingfield. Suddenly, he noticed the faces of the boys, all staring open-mouthed. Wingfield waved his arm. "James," he said, "go with those boys. Make yourself useful. Start gathering firewood. It is perfectly safe here," he added, glaring at Smith.

Smith started to object, but James blurted out, "Please, Master Wingfield, may I remove my shoes? Like Sam and Nate. I do think the sand is warm enough to keep me from getting a chill...."

"Yes, yes," Wingfield said. "I don't care if you take off your shoes. Just don't pester me with so many questions."

James looked as if he'd been slapped. "Begging your pardon, Master Wingfield," he said timidly. "I didn't mean to pester."

"Enough, James," Wingfield said. "You can go now."

When James stayed rooted to the spot, Wingfield roared, "Get out of my sight, James!"

Quickly, Sam tugged at the boy's sleeve. "Come on, James. I see some driftwood over there."

The three boys dashed across the sand, leaving Wingfield and Smith standing face to face in a war of angry looks.

~

On the third evening in the Canary Islands, Smith, Calthrop, and the three boys returned to the ship to find Captain Newport and Wingfield waiting.

"John Smith," the captain called in a clear, sharp voice. "You have been accused of mutiny. You are under arrest!" Four sailors surrounded Smith and bound his wrists together with ropes.

Sam ran to his master. The sailors brushed him aside.

"You will remain below until further notice," the captain said to Smith.

The color drained out of John Smith's face as he stared at Captain Newport. He clenched his jaw and shot a furious glance at Wingfield.

"Wait!" cried Calthrop. "What is going on? Captain, Master Edward, why has John been accused of mutiny? Who accuses him?"

The captain ignored Calthrop. He pointed to the ladder leading below deck, and two of the sailors took hold of the prisoner's arms. Captain Newport turned on his heel and marched off.

Sam watched helplessly as his master was led away.

"Master Edward, I demand to know what's going on here!" Calthrop shouted.

"I'm afraid you know only too well," Wingfield snarled. "And I warn you, Stephen. It is only your family connections that have spared you from arrest."

Calthrop glared at Wingfield.

"You were fortunate this time, Stephen. But take heed: Mutiny is a high crime, akin to treason." Wingfield pointed his finger at Calthrop. "If you persist in supporting that scoundrel John Smith, you may not be so fortunate in the future!"

~

A breeze off the ocean whipped the leaves of the trees and sprayed sand around the legs of the worshipers. The colonists strained to hear Reverend Hunt's words above the wind. Sam stood between Nate and James for the brief Sunday service before the fleet set sail from the Canary Islands.

Hunt led the colonists in two hymns and spoke of their duty to bring God's word to pagan shores. During his sermon, Hunt stopped several times to cough. Sam remembered sitting at Hunt's side when the ships were stalled off the coast of England and watching the minister cough, his body shaking with the effort. This morning, Hunt's coughing spells were brief, and he stood firm and straight.

Sam bowed his head respectfully, but his mind wasn't on the sermon. His eyes darted through the rows of gentlemen. John Smith was not among them, and Sam was keenly aware of his master's absence. He wondered how many of the others were also thinking about Smith. Sam studied the faces of the assembly, trying to guess each man's thoughts. He was convinced that Master Edward Wingfield was responsible for Smith's arrest. But which of the other men believed that Smith had plotted mutiny?

Dark thoughts crowded into Sam's head. *Mutiny is almost as bad as murder.* Sam frowned. He was certain that mutiny had never entered Master Smith's mind.

My master did quarrel with Master Wingfield. And my master made Captain Newport angry when Reverend Hunt was so sick. But mutiny? My master never plotted to seize control of the ship. A man would have to be desperate or crazy to even think of such a crime. Sam couldn't think of any reason for John Smith to feel desperate. And he knew perfectly well his master wasn't crazy.

Reverend Hunt closed the service with a prayer for the fleet's safe and speedy crossing of the Atlantic Ocean. The colonists headed toward the water's edge, where sailors waited to row them back to the ships.

Nate pulled at Sam's sleeve. Keeping his head bowed as if he were finishing a prayer, Nate whispered, "Master Calthrop has been ordered off the *Susan Constant*. We'll be sailing aboard the *Godspeed* instead." Nate's eyes glanced sideways at Sam. His voice cracked. "I shall be the only boy aboard that ship. If our ships get separated in a storm—"

Before Nate could finish, James interrupted. "You've been ordered off the *Susan Constant*?" he asked, amazed.

"Shhh!" Nate hissed, his eyes fastened on the sand. "I'm not supposed to speak of this. Master Wingfield wants my master separated from John Smith. He says Master Smith is a bad influence."

Sam stood stiffly on the beach. He groaned. Smith was under guard, and so far Sam hadn't been allowed near his master. Now his friend Nate would be sailing aboard another ship. That left white-faced, weak-bellied James as Sam's only companion on the voyage.

"What about that other boy?" James asked.

"What other boy?" Sam snapped. "Whatever are you talking about?"

"The fourth boy. The other page," James said. "A stout boy, with freckles. He's nearly as tall as a man. He's sailing on the smallest ship, the *Discovery*."

Nate frowned. "Now what good will it do me if there is a boy sailing on the *Discovery*? I'll still be the only boy on the *Godspeed*." Nate kicked the sand and trudged down the beach in search of Calthrop.

As Sam waited his turn for a place on the rowboats, he was only faintly aware of James chattering beside him. "Well, do you think you will tie yourself to the mast or not?" James said, his voice rising impatiently.

Sam stared at him. "Why would I want to tie myself to the mast? I don't know what you're talking about."

"You didn't listen!" complained James. "I was talking about a shipwreck. If the *Susan Constant* is wrecked, will you tie yourself to the mast to keep from washing into the sea? Or do you think it would be better to jump into the water and grab a floating board? If there are giant sea crabs, like the pictures on the maps, they could pick away your flesh while you're tied to the mast. But sea serpents could rear up from the deep and knock you off a floating board."

Giant sea crabs and serpents! Sam rolled his eyes. *No wonder James hates the sight of the sea—he actually believes those tales about the horrors of the deep!* It was only February 21—two months since the ships left England. *How many months,* Sam wondered, *will it take to reach Virginia?*

As soon as all the passengers were aboard and the longboat tied securely behind the *Susan Constant*, the sailors hauled up the huge, heavy anchor. They unfurled the ships' big white sails, and the voyage to the New World was underway.

Sam stood on the deck, enjoying the sun on his face and the wind ruffling his hair. He squinted across the water at the deck of the *Godspeed*. He fancied he could spot Nate. Sam waved, but nobody waved back. Truth was, Sam could hardly see a person on the distant ship. But the sight of the *Godspeed* and the *Discovery*—billowing white sails above sturdy brown hulls—lifted Sam's spirit. The ships populated the clear blue sky and gave Sam a feeling of companionship.

The next few days were long and dull for Sam. John Smith was a prisoner, and a sailor was assigned to guard him. Sam took Smith his daily portion of food and beer, but the guard ordered Sam away as soon as he delivered the meal. Smith's wrists were bound, and he did not look at Sam.

On the third day, Master Wingfield took charge and appointed passengers as guards. They were less strict. They let

Sam sit beside Smith as he spooned up his soup and chewed on his ship's biscuit. Smith ate his meal in silence. *The sparkle has gone out of my master's eyes,* Sam worried.

On the fourth day, Master Wingfield allowed Reverend Hunt to visit Smith. Sam stood quietly, holding a bowl of broth and some crusty biscuit, while Hunt prayed with the prisoner. Wingfield stood nearby and watched. He scowled when the minister made a few encouraging remarks after the prayer.

Except for the few moments each day when Sam attended Smith, the boy had no duties to keep him busy. Sometimes he climbed on deck looking for something to do. He was glad when the sailors asked him to scrub the deck or feed the chickens and pigs that were kept in wooden coops.

Sam spent hours staring across the waters. Molly, one of the ship's cats, took a liking to him and rubbed against his leg until he picked her up. She was striped black and gray, like most of the cats that lived in his family's barn. As he rubbed Molly's soft ears, Sam thought of his family. He tried to picture what each person would be doing. When he remembered his mother kneading dough by the kitchen fire, his eyes began to sting.

Quickly, he shifted his thoughts to his brother Thomas. How they used to race each other across the fields! Whenever there was an errand to run, they turned it into a competition. In the evenings by the fire, Sam and Thomas often had contests of strength—arm-wrestling or seeing who could hold a handstand the longest. Thomas was older and bigger than Sam, so he almost always won. But Sam was clever, and he used his wits to outsmart Thomas.

Once, Sam had suggested that they see who could climb higher in the big tree near the barn. Sam knew his smaller size and lighter weight would give him an advantage. But their father spotted them and shouted at them to come down. Oh, how he scolded Thomas—his firstborn son who was supposed to be learning the responsibilities of running the family farm—for letting Sam talk him into such a foolish contest!

Thinking about Thomas made Sam lonelier. He put the cat down and both of them prowled around the ship. The cook was usually willing to chat and always had a task for Sam to do. For helping, Sam was rewarded with an extra ship's biscuit.

For want of other companions, Sam sometimes sat with James on the 'tween deck. James had finally gotten used to the long, steady roll of the ship. He sometimes complained that his belly felt queasy, but he was able to keep down his share of hard biscuit and soup. He still refused to climb up to the deck, though, because the sight of the ocean frightened him.

Sitting in the dark, cramped quarters, the boys played games that required little space. One of the passengers let them play with a set of draughts, a board game that both boys had enjoyed in England. When they tired of that game, they had contests to see who could flip a button the farthest. Or they took turns hiding the button and played a guessing game to discover where it was hidden. Occasionally they shared stories about their families. James was barely eleven when he was sent to serve Master Wingfield. Both Sam and James had younger sisters, and they laughed about how silly girls were. Sometimes, the boys imagined aloud what they'd be doing if they were back at home. Sooner or later, thoughts of home and family made both boys feel gloomy.

One day, Sam suggested playing a game with words. "New," Sam called. He made up a line that ended with his word: "We cross the waves to find a world new." He looked at James.

James concentrated, his lips pursed. "We cross the waves to find a world new," he repeated, then added his own line to rhyme with Sam's. "A hundred settlers, not just a few."

Now it was Sam's turn. He repeated the two lines: "We cross the waves to find a world new. A hundred settlers, not just a few." Then he paused, concentrating. "The sky's our church, the ship's our pew."

"James!"

The boys looked up, startled.

Master Edward Wingfield called again, his voice impatient. "James! Where are you, lad?"

James scrambled to his feet. "Here I am. What shall I do for you, Master Wingfield?"

Sam edged into the shadows, hoping Master Wingfield would not notice him. He did not like to be under Wingfield's harsh gaze, and he suspected that Wingfield did not like to see him with James. As soon as James trotted off to do Master Wingfield's bidding, Sam climbed to the deck. He walked the length of the ship and inhaled great whiffs of the chilly sea air to clear his lungs of the stink of the dank, close sleeping quarters.

~

The fleet had been at sea three weeks when, one evening, the guard asked Sam if he'd like to sleep beside his master. Sam nodded eagerly and ran to get his blanket.

Sam flipped it open, stretched out on top of it, and rolled from one side to the other to make a woolen cocoon around himself. He strained to hear Smith's breathing. As soon as he was sure that his master was awake, Sam spoke. "What did she look like?"

Smith chuckled. "Who do you mean, Sam?"

"The Turkish lady," Sam said. "The princess. Remember that story you told me? About when you were captured and made a slave. Then you were given to that princess."

"Ah," Smith said. "She had hair as dark as midnight and her eyes were coal-black and gleaming, like the eyes of a wild animal."

Smith said slowly, as if he was looking at a picture and trying to find the words to describe it. "She wore heavy bracelets that jangled. Whenever she spoke, she waved her hands in the air. I could understand only a few words of her language. But when I watched her hands, I could sometimes tell her meaning."

"Did you think she was beautiful?" Sam asked. "You said she wanted to make you into a Turk so she could marry you. Would you have liked to marry her?"

Smith paused. When he continued, his voice was thoughtful. "No, Sam, I did not want to marry the heathen princess. But I wanted my freedom. So I watched her wave her small hands when she spoke. I studied her and I waited. At last, I found the moment to grab my freedom."

"How old did you say you were, Master Smith?" the guard asked. "When you were captured by the Turks?"

The guard is listening! Sam tensed. His master might be annoyed that the guard was eavesdropping, and Sam knew that if Smith was angry, he would refuse to talk.

"I was twenty-two when I was wounded in battle and taken captive by the Turks," Smith said quietly.

Sam waited, wondering if his master was going to continue. Molly jumped on Sam's tummy and turned around before curling up. She began to purr. If Smith did resume his story, Sam didn't hear it. It was comforting to be near his master again. The warmth of the cat soothed Sam's worries, and the rolling motion of the ship rocked him to sleep.

Sam awakened to the sound of Reverend Hunt's voice. "John, wake up! I have secured permission for you to walk on deck," Hunt said as he bent over Smith.

Sam sat up and rubbed his eyes. Hunt and Wingfield, both wearing coats, were standing between him and Smith. Sam caught Wingfield's eye and was greeted with a scowl.

Master Wingfield cleared his throat. "You will, of course, be escorted while you are on deck, Master Smith," he said. "You will refrain from conversation with the sailors and passengers.

I am understandably hesitant to allow so much liberty to a prisoner such as yourself. One who has been accused of such a serious crime. However, the good Reverend Hunt has appealed to my benevolent nature. Reverend Hunt is concerned that a long confinement will prove destructive to your physical health. Consequently, I have granted permission for a brief walk on deck. Your own conduct will determine whether my generosity will be repeated on a future occasion."

Smith opened his mouth to reply, but Reverend Hunt held up his hand. "I believe the brisk morning air is most healthful, John," he said quickly. "So I recommend that you dress yourself immediately."

Wingfield led the way, with Reverend Hunt behind him. When they reached the open deck, Hunt walked beside Smith. The guard followed close behind the prisoner, and Sam took up the rear. Each man wore a coat, the collars drawn up to shield their faces from the wind. Nobody spoke. The sailors stared at them. *This is like a funeral march,* Sam thought. Master Wingfield nodded when he passed Captain Newport. The captain returned the nod then looked away.

Without waiting to be invited, Sam spread out his blanket beside his master again that night. The next morning, Hunt and Wingfield came to take the prisoner for another walk on deck, and Sam again followed behind.

Each night, Sam thought his master's voice grew stronger as he recounted adventures from his youthful travels. Each morning as they climbed to the deck and breathed the brisk sea air, Sam thought Smith's step grew firmer. Although Wingfield continued to oversee the morning walks, the prisoner gave him no cause for alarm. Smith made no attempt to speak with sailors or other passengers. *My master is waiting and watching,* Sam noted. *He's studying how to please Master Wingfield and the captain so he can regain his freedom.*

Nearly every afternoon before the meal was served, Hunt came to pray with the prisoner. Wingfield did not always remain by the clergyman's side during these prayers. *Master Wingfield has begun to trust John Smith,* Sam thought happily. *Any day now, Captain Newport will surely order the guard to release my master.* When Sam ate beside him, Smith talked and smiled. He chatted pleasantly with his guards.

One day, after Sam had taken Smith his evening meal, he went up on deck. A fair wind was blowing the *Susan Constant* across the water. The weather seemed to be smiling on the small fleet, and the sun glittered on deck. It was warm enough for Sam to roll up his shirtsleeves as he leaned on the rail to watch the glow of the evening sunset.

The West Indies

L and ho!"

When Sam heard the call from the sailor on the topmast, he scrambled up the ladder and raced to the railing. It was March 23, nearly a month after the fleet had left the Canary Islands. Far to the west, Sam could see a gray shadow topped by clouds on the horizon. Captain Newport announced that their ship was fourteen degrees north of the equator, near an island in the West Indies called Martinique. As the shadow slowly rose up from the sea, Sam could distinguish mountains poking into the clouds. A bright spit of sand appeared, framed by emerald green bushes and slender palm trees. Sam's muscles tingled at the sight of land. All that space! He was eager to feel the sand beneath his toes, to stretch his legs and run along that beach.

The three ships continued sailing, and the next morning they reached an island called Dominica and dropped anchor. The longboat was brought around, and Captain Newport ordered some of the sailors to row ashore with barrels to fill with fresh water. Sam asked permission to go with the sailors, and the captain smiled and nodded.

Sam scrambled down into the longboat. The sun glinted off the surface of the water, making shimmery reflections. A pleasant breeze rustled the leaves of tall palm trees leaning over the beach. Sam took off his shirt, then his shoes. He wrapped his shirt around the shoes and tied the sleeves together. As soon as the boat grounded on the sand, he tumbled into the surf, holding his bundle above the waves.

The salty water woke up the skin on his feet. Sam rubbed wet sand over his ankles, scouring off weeks of grime. When he reached the beach, he peeled off his wet britches and threw them and his bundle of clothes on the damp sand. He splashed back into the surf and stuck his head under the clear aqua water. He scrubbed his skin and hair with scoops of sand and saltwater.

Sam brought up handfuls of shiny shells from the ocean floor. The shells sparkled in the sunshine, and Sam thought them more beautiful than rubies or sapphires.

Kicking his legs as he ran through the shallows, Sam sent up sprays of water. When he tired of running, he threw himself on the sand and let the warm sun and gentle breeze dry his skin. The earth beneath him was solid, and the sky seemed endless. Sam inhaled the clean air, the salty smell of the sea mixing with the wonderful fragrance of green plants that grew along the edge of the sand.

Another rowboat approached the beach. Sam sat up and squinted, searching for Nate's face. When he didn't see his friend, Sam splashed slowly through the blue-green water. Schools of colorful fish darted away when he approached.

At last, he heard a loud whistle. Sam squinted at a rowboat in the deeper water. This time, he spotted Nate waving his arms and shouting.

Sam waded into the waves. Nate was sitting in the boat beside Stephen Calthrop, and both of them were grinning. "Look, Nate," said Calthrop, pointing at Sam, "a heathen boy is come to greet you. Naked as the day he was born!" Calthrop chuckled.

Nate tugged off his shoes, stripped off his shirt, and jumped out of the rowboat. The boat rocked, and water splashed on some of the men. None of the gentlemen complained—they were as delighted to be off the ship as the boys.

Bobbing up and down in the waves, Nate turned to Sam and said, "Race you to the beach!"

Sam began to push his way through the water, but movements on the beach caught his eye. Sam stared. Strange-looking men were coming out of the trees! Nate knelt beside Sam in the shallows, and both boys strained to see and hear.

Unlike the Englishmen, the strangers' faces were as smooth as children's, with no beards or mustaches. They were naked, and their brown skin was painted red. Designs of a deeper color were tattooed on their faces, arms, and chests. When the strangers turned, Sam could see that their hair was braided into three long plaits that hung down their backs to their waists.

Some of the sailors approached the natives and made gestures with their hands. A sailor lifted a wooden barrel, then held up his hands as if he were drinking from a cup.

One of the natives pointed at the ships.

The sailors turned toward the east, and one of them swept out his arm in a large arc to show how far their ships had come across the ocean.

The natives nodded. Some of them surrounded the rowboats. Their dark hands cupped the metal oar fittings and felt the smooth planks. They chattered as they examined the boat. Sam couldn't hear the words they were saying.

Sam looked at the natives' muscular arms and legs. "They don't have beards like our sailors, but they don't look like children," he whispered to Nate. "They're tall and broad-chested." Sam stared at the weapons the natives carried, and his stomach muscles tightened. "Their spears don't look like children's toys, either!"

When the natives turned and walked into the trees, Sam let out a sigh of relief. "Do you think they'll come back and attack?" he asked Nate.

Nate shrugged. "They didn't shout or threaten the sailors with their spears. Our men haven't even started to load their muskets." He grinned. "I guess these natives are peaceful enough."

The boys waded to the beach and flopped onto the packed sand. "How was the crossing aboard the *Susan Constant?*" Nate asked. "Is Master Smith still a prisoner?"

"Yes, but not for long, I think. At first, I wasn't allowed near him. But now I sleep beside him. And I go along when Reverend Hunt takes him for walks on deck every morning. I think Captain Newport will set him free any day."

While the boys talked, the rowboat from the smallest ship, *Discovery*, approached the beach. A young fellow hopped out and helped drag the boat out of the water. He was as tall and stocky as a man, but his face was smooth like a boy's.

The fellow looked around, then headed for Sam and Nate. His stride was long and sure. He pointed at his chest with his thumb and said, "Name's Richard Mutton. I sailed aboard the *Discovery*. I'm the page of Master George Kendall."

So this is the fourth boy, thought Sam, *the one James told us about.*

"Nate Peacock," said Nate, shaking the fellow's hand. "And this is Sam Collier. I'm the page of Stephen Calthrop. And Sam here—"

"I've heard," Richard interrupted. "He serves the criminal, John Smith. My master told me about him," Richard said. "Aboard the *Discovery*, they're saying there'll be a hanging soon. What's the use of bringing a criminal into our new colony? As it is, we'll be surrounded by murderous, heathen savages. We needn't bring a man we can't trust to live in our own settlement with us."

Sam glared. "My master's arrest was a mistake," he said. "He's no criminal. He never plotted a mutiny."

Richard sneered. "Tell that to the hangman," he snorted.

Sam balled his hands into fists. "I said Master Smith was arrested by mistake," he growled. "He's no criminal, and you better not call him that again. My master will be released any day!"

"Sure he'll be released. On a gallows!" Richard gave Sam a nasty smile and puffed out his chest.

Nate stepped beside Sam. "Look here, Richard Mutton. You don't know Master Smith or anything about what happened." Nate's voice was even. "It was a mistake, that's all. If Sam says his master is going to be released any day...well, he ought to know. After all, he's sailing aboard the *Susan Constant*. And Captain Newport is the admiral in charge of our whole fleet. So there's no point quarreling. You just heard some things that weren't true."

Richard smirked. "We'll see."

The three boys joined the sailors and helped them carry the water barrels into the woods beyond the beach. Sam didn't speak another word to Richard Mutton the rest of the day.

～

The fleet sailed to the island of Nevis, which had plenty of fresh water. Captain Newport said it looked like a promising place to hunt. "We'll make camp here for a few days," he told the passengers. "While I send out some hunters, you may rest and refresh yourselves on land."

The sailors pulled the longboat around. Before allowing anyone to board the smaller craft, Captain Newport ordered two crewmen to bring John Smith on deck. The captain looked at the crowd of passengers and announced, "I have decided to release this man. His conduct during the crossing has convinced me that this is a reasonable course of action."

Wingfield watched, stiff and silent, as the sailors cut the ropes that bound Smith. Smith rubbed the red, raw skin on his wrists. He smiled at Reverend Hunt, then nodded at the captain and Wingfield.

Beaming, Hunt rushed to Smith's side and clapped his hands on Smith's shoulders.

Wingfield didn't move. "You are released from confinement, Mister Smith," he said. "But not entirely from suspicion. It would be wise for you to remember that there are ample supplies of rope on this ship."

Smith's eyes met Wingfield's. To Sam's relief, his master did not reply. Instead, Smith climbed over the rail and stepped down into the longboat. Sam followed.

As the sailors rowed them ashore, the sun shone on Sam's face. A light breeze stirred the tips of his hair. Sam couldn't think of anything that would make the day more perfect. *Captain Newport says we have a few days to explore this beautiful island. Then, on to Virginia!* Sam thought. *And my master is free!* A smile spread across his face.

While they camped on Nevis, the colonists sorted themselves into two groups. One group, which included Stephen Calthrop, surrounded Smith and congratulated him. The other group, which included Richard Mutton's master, George Kendall, turned their backs on Smith and his friends.

Although they were not willing to speak to Smith, the men in the second group often spoke about him. When Sam walked by Smith's enemies, their conversation halted. Sam knew these men were saying things about his master that they didn't want him to hear. Richard Mutton avoided Sam's glance and pretended that he'd never introduced himself.

But the island of Nevis was too intriguing for Sam to dwell on the bad feelings among the grown men. Around the campfires, Sam had his first taste of pelican, parrot, and iguana meat. He especially liked the roasted pelican, and he sat near the campfire stuffing himself, meat juices running down his chin.

Hunting parties brought back alligators and piled them into heaps on the sand. Sam, Nate, and James examined the dead creatures closely. The hides felt hard and scaly, and the long teeth made Sam shiver.

James wrinkled his nose in disgust and refused to taste cooked alligator. "I'm not going to put the flesh of that loathsome beast in my mouth!" he declared.

~

Both the *Godspeed* and the *Discovery* had developed leaks during the ocean crossing, and the sailors set to work patching their hulls. After several days on Nevis, Captain Newport decided to take the *Susan Constant* to explore some of the nearby islands while the repairs on the smaller vessels were being completed.

The *Susan Constant* sailed to the Isle of Virgins. In the waters around this island, the sailors caught large sea turtles, enough to feed eighty men for three days. With the hold filled with sea turtles, Captain Newport ordered the ship to return to Nevis to rejoin the others.

The clear blue sky reflected off the shimmering water. It was a beautiful day for sailing.

Sam leaned against the railing to watch the green islands pass by. James stood next to him. The younger boy's face was sunburned, and tiny flakes of peeling skin dotted his forehead. He inhaled great whiffs of fresh air. "The air in these islands is a blessing," he said. "I believe it was worth braving the horrid ocean to stand on this deck today."

Sam grinned. He would not have chosen the word "braving" to describe James aboard ship or shore!

"Land ho!" called the lookout. "The island of Nevis!"

The passengers crowded onto the deck to watch as their ship approached the shore. John Smith, smiling broadly, moved forward and stood beside Sam.

When the *Susan Constant* glided past the other two ships, Sam waved and shouted. A wooden structure was standing on the beach. A tall, dark structure. Sam squinted at it. *What is that?*

The sailors released the ship's anchor into the water, sending up a splash.

Smith gasped. Sam followed his master's eyes and stared again at the wooden structure. Now he recognized what it was—a gallows!

As soon as the sailors readied the longboat, Captain Newport climbed into it. Master Wingfield and Reverend Hunt took their places beside the captain. Without asking permission, John Smith followed, his face grim.

Sam clambered down after his master. His mind was racing. *A gallows! Who's going to be hanged?* Richard Mutton's words kept crowding into his head, but Sam tried to brush them away. *Those gallows can't be for my master!* he assured himself. The sun beat down fiercely on Sam's neck, but his hands felt icy cold. He tried to breathe calmly, to think of another logical explanation. *Could one of the natives on Nevis have attacked an Englishman?* As the longboat neared the shore, Sam could see Stephen Calthrop standing among the sailors and passengers from the *Godspeed* and *Discovery* who were assembled on the beach.

Calthrop hurried to Smith's side when the boat's passengers stepped into the shallows. "I don't know what's got into them, John," Calthrop said quietly. "I didn't even know that anything was afoot until last night. Kendall and some of the others have talked this lot into a frenzy. They claim you're guilty of mutiny and should be hanged before we reach Virginia. They're saying there are too many dangers in the wilderness without us bringing a criminal into our colony."

Captain Newport, Master Wingfield, and Reverend Hunt quickly joined the other two ships' captains and some of the gentlemen who were huddled on the beach. It was obvious that they were talking about Smith, because they turned and pointed

Sam stared at the wooden structure. It was a gallows!

at him as they spoke. They made no effort to keep their voices down. Sam could hear shouted words above the sound of the waves crashing on the beach.

"Gentlemen, we are civilized men. Englishmen!" Reverend Hunt's voice rose above the others. "Until it is proven that a crime has been committed, we do not punish the accused." Hunt swung around and glared at each man standing on the beach. "Who among ye hath proof of John Smith's guilt?"

Except for the sounds of the wind and the surf, the beach grew silent. Nobody stepped forward to offer evidence against Smith.

Hunt's voice thundered as if he stood in a pulpit delivering a sermon. "Hath ye traveled to a distant shore to lay aside the teachings of church and country and become heathens? Hath ye bid farewell to Mother Reason as well as Mother England?" The minister's eyes were blazing. "Shall ye colonize the New World as proud subjects of King James? As Christian men? Or shall ye strip off these English garments and become savages?"

One by one, the men lowered their eyes. After a long silence, Captain Newport ordered two of the sailors to dismantle the gallows. Then he looked at Smith, who met his gaze without blinking. The captain cleared his throat and announced that the fleet would be leaving the island of Nevis the next morning.

Sam's knees were wobbling, and he sank onto the sand. Before leaving England, he had heard many tales about the dangers of this journey. He had heard about sea serpents lurking deep in the ocean. About naked savages who howled like wolves. About fierce winds that blew ships over the edge of the earth. Sam had suspected that these tales were all nonsense, and he was right. None of them had proven true. Yet there were dangers that Sam had never considered. His countrymen had built a gallows and planned to hang one of their own Englishmen!

~

The fleet set off again on April 4 and sailed around a large island with jagged mountains surrounded by green forests. On the seventh of April, the ships reached a much smaller island, called Mona. Captain Newport wanted to replenish their food and fresh water before leaving the West Indies, but he was nervous about the reports he'd heard about Mona's natives. Newport selected a group of gentlemen as a landing party and ordered them to get iron helmets and breastplates and assemble on deck.

As Sam and James helped the sailors carry weapons on deck, they listened to Newport briefing the landing party. "Gentlemen, there are reports that Mona's natives have attacked English sailors."

James shuddered and glanced at Sam. The sun was already high in the sky, and Sam felt sweat roll down his back.

"The natives are clever," Newport continued. "They wait until the Englishmen leave the safety of their ship's cannons. They use poisoned arrows, so it's important that you wear your armor at all times when you leave our ship. Each of you will carry a gun and a sword, and you should be prepared to use them." Newport paused and looked at the faces of the men. "If we are attacked, we must fight to the death, gentlemen. These natives are cannibals. They eat the flesh of the men they capture." James dropped the iron helmet he was carrying.

The gentlemen began to mutter among themselves.

Sam edged close to James and whispered, "Cap'n Newport said the natives are afraid of our cannons, James. We'll be safe aboard the ship. And don't worry about the landing party—the gentlemen are wearing heavy armor. Nothing will happen to them."

Newport ordered all hands and the other passengers to remain on the ships until the landing party returned.

The sunny morning turned into a sweltering day. Sam and James stayed on deck, preferring the scorching tropical sun to the baking heat below.

At dusk, Captain Newport and the others returned to the beach, and the sailors rowed out to get them. Sam and James watched as the men unloaded two wild boars and some iguanas on deck. They were surprised to see them bring aboard an extra set of armor. The boys listened as one of the men explained that the armor belonged to Edward Brooks, who had collapsed and died during their six-mile march through the jungle.

"Edward's fat melted within him because of the island's great heat. We were not able to relieve him," the man said. "Indeed, many of us were fainting in the march and thought to die alongside him. Considering the great extremity of the countryside, I think it good fortune that only one of our party was lost."

James turned to Sam, his eyes wide. Sam heard his own heart pounding in his chest. *An Englishman is dead and buried,* he thought, *and our ships have not even reached Virginia!* Sam liked to say that he was never going to return to England, but he hadn't thought of dying in this new world.

~

They set sail again, and two days later, the ships reached the island of Monito. Captain Newport ordered the sailors to drop anchor, and John Smith, Master Wingfield, and several other gentlemen volunteered to go ashore. Sam asked if he could go with his master, and Captain Newport nodded.

Wingfield beckoned for James to follow him into the longboat. Although James hesitated at first, he got into the longboat and sat beside his master.

For nearly an hour, sailors maneuvered the small craft along Monito's coastline, looking for a place to approach the shore. Waves slammed the boat around wildly, threatening to dash it against the sharp boulders jutting out from the island. James edged away from the side of the boat, and his knuckles turned white as he clutched the seat.

After several attempts, the sailors finally reached a stony ledge, and the passengers scrambled out and struggled up a steep, rocky slope. The sound of the pounding surf wiped out all other noise until they reached the top. When at last they entered a grassy meadow framed by bushes and trees, Sam was astonished by the racket. Thousands of birds surrounded them. As he tramped through the grass, birds' eggs smashed under his feet. Brightly colored little birds hopped and darted out of his way. Overhead, birds flew as thick as hail. Their twittering made it nearly impossible for the Englishmen to converse.

The party entered the woods, and John Smith positioned himself beside a bush. Birds chattered in the branches, hopping only inches from his arms. Suddenly Smith grabbed one, snapped its neck with a twist, and dropped it into a sack. The others followed Smith's lead. Standing quietly beside the bushes, each man could catch a bird every few minutes.

Sam and James imitated Smith's technique and found the birds surprisingly easy to catch. Sam caught three of the little birds and twisted their necks, but he did feel sorry when the pretty creatures went limp. Unlike the chickens on his family's farm, these birds were as colorful as embroidered pictures. He made another grab and missed. Nearby, James caught one bird after another, snapped their necks, and tossed them into a pile at his feet. James's small hands moved as swiftly as owls swooping after field mice.

In a few hours, their group collected enough of the little birds to fill up two barrels.

That evening, the cook prepared the birds, skewered them on sticks, and passed them out to the colonists, who roasted them over fires. Each tiny bird was only a few mouthfuls, but the meat was soft and tender.

That night, when Sam curled up on his blankets, he ran his tongue along his teeth to dislodge the bits of roasted meat. Molly, the ship's cat, hopped on top of him. She kneaded his side, pricking him with her claws. As soon as the cat settled down, Sam closed his eyes. He thought about how the longboat had nearly been wrecked on the sharp rocks of Monito. Picturing the island's colorful, noisy birds, he drifted into a fuzzy sleep. In his mind, he was sailing toward a sparkling island—rocky and full of dangers. The images blended until the island took flight and became a bird soaring above the ocean, above billowing white sails on sturdy brown ships. Sam wheeled in a great arc and saw a dark gallows on sparkling sands. As he approached, natives began to shoot poison-tipped arrows. The Englishmen couldn't fight back because they were boiling to death inside their armor.

Sam jerked awake. Sweat oozed down his chest. He shook his head to clear away the nightmare's frightening images. Molly nuzzled his hand.

When I was a small boy, Father often praised me for my courage, Sam thought. *I've never been afraid of the dark. Or of high places. I didn't feel the least bit frightened when Father told me that he was sending me to serve a man named John Smith, who would take me across the sea to a land that few Englishmen have ever seen.*

But deep inside, Sam knew that his nightmare was about fear. He was afraid of Virginia, afraid of dying. Sam rolled onto his back and lifted Molly onto his chest. He stroked her back and ran his fingers along her tail.

For the first time in his life, Sam admitted to himself that he was scared. He didn't like the feeling. He vowed he would not let himself become a coward. "No matter what happens in Virginia," he whispered, "I will face it bravely."

Virginia

On April 10, 1607, the ships left the islands and sailed north into open waters. Four days later, Captain Newport plotted their latitude and announced they were leaving the tropics surrounding the equator. Now the fleet would be sailing into cooler waters.

A week later, the wind picked up and the afternoon sky darkened. Thunder boomed, and rain pelted the ship. The sailors hurried to reef the sails and close the hatches. The *Susan Constant* began to heave and plunge on ocean swells, which rose higher and higher until they actually towered over the ship's masts. Captain Newport struggled to steer into the wind and waves. If a wall of water hit the ship broadside, she would overturn and sink.

Below, the colonists scrambled to lash down loose objects. Two lanterns swung wildly, casting a flickering light over their efforts. When the ship lurched, Sam and the other passengers had to grab for the beams or heavy trunks to keep from colliding. Great waves were splashing onto the deck, and seawater leaked through the hatches and spilled down below. Soon their clothing was soaked.

Shivering, Sam crouched beside James and tried to reassure him. "The *Susan Constant* will ride out this storm, James," he said. Sam hoped his voice sounded more confident than he felt.

"This is a good, stout ship. Storms happen at sea all the time, but sailors live to be just as old as anyone else." Sam's words had a calming effect on himself, but James looked as scared as a lost puppy.

The sea was crashing against the ship's hull, and the wind screamed. "Listen to me, James!" Sam shouted to be heard over the storm. "The captain knew we might run into storms. That's why our fleet left England in wintertime—so we could reach Virginia before the hurricane season. And we're almost there. Master Smith says we've traveled in a great arc, following the trade winds. First we went south and passed the western coast of Africa, where the Canary Islands are. Then we swung across the Atlantic and passed the West Indies. We're heading north now, James. We should be in Virginia in a few days."

Suddenly the *Susan Constant* pitched violently to one side. Water sloshed over the boys' knees. James vomited and began to sob.

The storm blew for days. When the wind and rain finally let up, Captain Newport feared they'd been blown far off course. But several days later, on the morning of the twenty-sixth of April, John Smith nudged Sam's shoulder to awaken him. "The sailors have spotted land!" Smith said.

Sam sat up quickly. "Is it Virginia?" he asked, his voice trembling with excitement.

"Aye, lad. That's what the captain is saying."

Sam sprang to his feet and followed his master up to the open deck. The sky was just changing from gray to pink. Holding onto the ship's rail, Sam looked where Smith pointed and saw a long, low brownish shape on the distant horizon. "That's North America, Sam," Smith said.

Slowly the ships entered the Bay of Chesapeake. Sam and the other Englishmen watched the morning sun introduce this glorious new world. As the details of the distant shore took shape, the colonists were amazed to see immense trees and lush green forests.

"Have you ever seen such stout, healthy trees?" a gentleman named George Percy exclaimed. "Why, a man could build a sturdy house from the wood of just one of those trees!" He began to weep. "I am almost ravished at the sight," he cried out.

Sam looked at Smith, alarmed. He had never seen a grown man cry so openly.

Smith smiled and whispered, "Master Percy fancies himself a man of letters, Sam. His feelings are an open book. Men who scribble their emotions onto paper have less need to hide their tears from other men."

Captain Newport watched for a good place to land. Soon the ships were riding at anchor, and the sailors rowed the colonists to shore. Sam scrambled onto the muddy ground and let his eyes feast on the beauty in every direction. The sun was shining and the air was pleasantly warm. White seabirds cawed and wheeled above, as if they were welcoming him to his new home. He sniffed. The smell of decaying plants and new life reminded him of the marshes around Lincolnshire. Small crabs scuttled through seeping puddles in the mud. Sam reached out a finger to touch tiny white shell creatures clinging to the tips of bright green grasses.

"Is this Virginia? For certain?" he asked.

"Yes, Sam, this is Virginia," Smith said, beaming. "Isn't it magnificent!"

The colonists explored the grassy marshland and wandered into the forest. At dusk, they gathered at the shore to wait for the sailors to row them back to the ships. Suddenly, Sam heard a rustling from the trees. He turned to see natives creeping toward them on all fours. In the gray light the natives looked like smooth-haired bears to Sam. They carried bows in their

*Arrows slammed into the mud around him. Sam heard the
screams of wounded men.*

mouths and arrows in pouches slung over their backs. When some of the gentlemen shouted in alarm, the natives leaped to their feet. As they charged at the Englishmen, the Indians yelled and whooped.

Arrows rained through the air while the colonists fumbled to prime their muskets. Only a few of the gentlemen were carrying the burning rope matches needed to fire their muskets. John Smith was one of these few, and he raised his gun to shoot.

"Get down, Sam!" Smith commanded as he emptied a cylinder of powder into his gun and reached for more lead shot.

Sam crouched and covered his head with his arms. Arrows slammed into the mud around him. He heard the screams of wounded men.

After a few of the Englishmen fired their guns, the natives fled into the trees. Sam rose slowly. One of the gentlemen, Gabriel Archer, had blood all over his hands where arrows had grazed his fingers. Some of the men washed Archer's wounds and bound strips of cloth around his hands.

A sailor had been wounded more seriously. He lay on the ground moaning. Sam watched as Smith and some of the others crouched over him and yanked out two arrows. The sailor screamed when the arrow points were torn out. But Smith said the wounds were not deep. He stuffed cloth into the punctures to stop the bleeding and told the men to carry the sailor aboard one of the rowboats.

Sam pulled an arrow out of the mud before hopping into the longboat. He stuck it into his waistband so he could examine it in the safety of the ship. As the longboat neared the *Susan Constant,* Sam thought about the tales he'd heard about the natives of Virginia. They were said to be gentle, childlike people who were eager to welcome newcomers to their prosperous land. *That's a lie,* Sam thought grimly. *The natives attacked us on our first day in Virginia. They're not gentle children. And they don't want us here.*

Sam sat on his blanket and examined the arrow. He ran his index finger over its sharpened stone point and its straight shaft. Bird feathers had been trimmed and fastened with animal sinew onto the shaft. He tossed the arrow and watched how straight it flew. Sam had tried shooting with bow and arrows in Lincolnshire, and he recognized the skill that had produced this arrow.

~

In the morning, Captain Newport announced that a crew would go ashore and begin assembling their shallop, a boat designed to explore shallow coastal waters. The parts for the shallop had been stored in the Susan Constant's hold during the crossing. To guard against another attack, Newport ordered some men to put on their armor and get their weapons ready. The sailors rowed these guards ashore before they returned to ferry across the parts for the shallop.

When the shallop was ready, Captain Newport decided to take a short exploring trip to try it out. George Percy was one of the gentlemen chosen to go. When the group returned, Percy gave a detailed account of what he had seen. "Our party ventured across a flat expanse of mud. Wherever our boots trod, we discovered mussels. The shallow water, which was as clear as the air we breathe, was full of fine oysters—so numerous were they, as stones in a field!" Percy opened his hand and showed off pearls, which he had found in the oysters. "We came into a little plat of ground full of fine and beautiful strawberries, four times bigger and better than ours in England," Percy said.

Sam was sitting with Nate and James as Percy spoke. The boys looked at each other, their eyes sparkling at the thought of juicy strawberries and shining pearls. *Oh, I cannot wait to explore this new world!* Sam thought.

The explorers had taken the shallop to a flat shoulder of land. They named that spot Cape Henry, and Reverend Hunt set up a cross there. On April 30, Captain Newport ordered the three sailing ships to move upriver to that cape.

At Cape Henry, Captain Newport opened the sealed box containing the instructions from the Virginia Company. He reminded the passengers of their mission: Gather Virginia timber, furs, and foods for sale in England. Search for gold and precious stones. Explore Virginia's rivers to find an easy water route across the continent so ships could sail from England to the Orient for silk and spices. Teach the Protestant religion to the natives. John Smith had already explained all these tasks to Sam.

But Sam was as surprised as the others when he heard the rest of the company's instructions. These were directions for governing the colony after Captain Newport returned to England. The company had written that a six-man ruling council should be left in charge. In the sealed box were the names of the men appointed to this council: Bartholomew Gosnold and John Ratcliffe, captains of the *Godspeed* and the *Discovery*, and three gentlemen, Edward Wingfield, John Martin, and George Kendall. The sixth member was John Smith!

When Smith's name was read aloud, the colonists gasped. John Smith was not a highborn Englishman like the others! In England, people were born into a class of society, and only men from the highest class were supposed to be leaders. The English settlers assumed that family status would determine who ruled their colony, as well.

"Why did the Virginia Company appoint a man of Smith's middling status to our council?" the colonists muttered to one another. "Shouldn't the members of our ruling committee be men from the best families, like the ruling bodies of England?"

"Smith was never cleared of the charge of mutiny," one man grumbled. "He's a criminal! We can't trust him to govern our colony."

Sam kept his eyes on his master's face as the colonists broke into a shouting match. John Smith looked straight ahead, his mouth locked in stony silence. His hands were clenched as if he could hold down his temper with his fingers.

Master Wingfield was in a fury. He jabbed at the air with his finger as he spoke to the men beside him. George Kendall, Richard Mutton's master, pounded his fist into his open hand and shouted. All the gentlemen were trying to voice their opinions at the same time. When Sam could distinguish what they were saying, he realized they were insulted because Smith had been elevated above them—this meant Smith would command men whose social status was higher than his own.

The laborers also objected, but for a different reason. They were upset because the social order that they had always accepted was being changed. Already nervous about moving to an unexplored wilderness so far from home, the laborers were frightened by Smith's appointment. In England, common men didn't govern. How could their colony succeed if a commoner was put in charge?

Not a single voice spoke in favor of putting Smith on the council—not even Stephen Calthrop's or Reverend Hunt's.

Sam caught Nate's eye, and Nate shrugged as if to say that he couldn't understand how this new trouble had happened. Both boys knew that such arguments could turn deadly. *The last time the colonists turned against my master, they built a gallows on the beach!* Sam thought.

After several polite attempts to calm the group, Captain Newport roared, "Gentlemen! Come to order!"

At last, the commotion faded. Newport continued, "As fleet commander, I am in charge here. And I am going to override the company's instructions. John Smith will not take his place on the council."

Now Sam was completely confused. *How can they remove my master from the council?* he wondered. *Surely it isn't lawful to disobey the company's instructions.* Sam glanced at his master. Only Smith's flushed cheeks showed his feelings. Sam remembered the look on his master's face when Wingfield scolded him on the beach in the Canary Islands. He remembered how tense Smith had become when Master Calthrop repeated the captain's remarks about his social status and lack of manners. *He's very angry,* Sam thought. *John Smith is always angry when his social class is mentioned.*

After Newport resolved the issue of Smith's appointment to the council, he explained the company's directions for choosing the first president of the colony. The ruling councilmen would select one man from their members. The new council chose Master Wingfield, and none of the colonists objected. Wingfield came from a powerful, aristocratic family. He had relatives in the highest ranks of England's government. He was exactly the type of man expected to command Englishmen.

The fleet set sail again to explore the northern side of the river. When the sailors spotted five natives running along the riverbank, Captain Newport put on armor and ordered a crew to row him ashore. He called to the natives, who seemed frightened until the captain laid his hand over his heart. Then the natives set their bows and arrows on the ground and approached. Using signs, the natives invited the newcomers to visit their town, which they called Kecoughtan.

The captain sent for a party of sailors and gentlemen to accompany him to the Indian town. John Smith offered to go, and Sam went along.

The town of Kecoughtan was within a stone's throw of the river. While the Englishmen pulled the shallop onto the beach, the natives gathered to watch. They lay facedown on the ground, scratched the earth with their fingers, and moaned loudly.

"Why are they scratching the dirt?" Sam asked John Smith. "Is that the way these people greet visitors?"

"I don't know, Sam," Smith replied. "My guess is that they're praying to us. As if they think we are gods come to their village."

Sam hoped the natives did not consider it rude to stare, because he could not take his eyes off them. Apparently, it was not their custom to cover their bodies with clothing. Except for leather pieces tied on strings around their waists, both men and women wore nothing but red or black paint. The men scraped the hair off one side of their heads, so it would not get caught in their bowstrings. The long hair on the other side was braided and decorated with feathers. Birds' bones hung through holes in their earlobes.

The Kecoughtans spread out woven mats and invited their guests to sit. Sam sat behind John Smith and helped himself to a small cake from one of the bowls passed around by the villagers. It tasted like a moist, mealy loaf of bread. The Indians also served cooked meat, which Sam ate with relish.

While they ate, Sam looked back and forth from the Indians to the Englishmen. The colonists were dressed in their usual clothing—long-sleeved shirts covered by waistcoats, breeches, woolen stockings, and leather shoes. Beads of sweat rolled down their noses and hung in their heavy beards.

Sam had left off his waistcoat and stockings and rolled up his shirtsleeves. Since he was just a boy, Master Smith had not objected when he imitated the sailors and left his shirt open at the chest. But Sam still felt uncomfortable. It was already as hot as full summer in England. And Virginia's humidity made the spring air feel sticky. Sam began to wish he could strip off the rest of his clothing and go naked, like the Indians.

After the feast, the Indians staged an entertainment for their guests. One brave stood and clapped his hands. Others danced in a circle around him, stamping their feet and shouting. Some of the dancers scowled fiercely and let out piercing screams, which made Sam jump. A few dancers howled like wolves or pawed the air like bears.

Sam and the other Englishmen watched the dancing for about a half-hour. Then Captain Newport stood up and presented beads as gifts to the dancers before leading the colonists back to their ship for the night.

The English fleet continued up the broad river, which was lined with grassy banks and some spits of sand. Several feet from shore, Sam could see scrubby bushes and small trees, with forest beyond. He longed to be off the ship and out exploring in those woods.

Finally the ships dropped anchor at a promising spot, where the soil supported sturdy trees and thick, green undergrowth. Captain Newport sent out a landing party, and the men returned with reports of abundant wildlife—deer, squirrels, rabbits, colorful little songbirds, and much larger gamebirds.

Gabriel Archer, the gentleman whose hands had been injured in the first Indian attack, urged Captain Newport to remain here. "Truly, this is as goodly a place as we're likely to come upon, Captain. An abundance of sturdy trees. Game a'plenty. Rich soil that invites seed to grow."

But the captain hesitated. "I don't know, Gabriel. I'm not satisfied," Newport said. "It's not safe. The river is too shallow by the shore. Our ships will be forced to anchor too far out in the river—away from our settlement. We'll be in constant danger of attack by the natives or by Spanish vessels coming up from the bay."

Master Wingfield agreed. He argued that the colonists needed the safety offered by their ships in this dangerous new world. After all, one of their men had mysteriously dropped dead in the West Indies, and natives had attacked them on their first night in Virginia.

The other settlers agreed, too. The ships—with their thick hulls and iron cannons mounted for battle—provided safety against the unknown. So the sailors pulled up anchor and the search continued. Before leaving the point, Captain Newport declared he would name it Archer's Hope in honor of Gabriel Archer, who had argued in favor of settling there.

The next day, on May 13, the ships came to a large tract of land that jutted into the deeper part of the river. Captain Newport ordered the ships to pull in close to shore. At this spot, the ships could practically touch the bank. A settlement here would be far enough upstream to be safe from a surprise attack by the Spanish. The sailors moored the ships to the trees, and Captain Newport sent a party of gentlemen to explore the riverbank.

That evening, Captain Newport called the colonists together and announced that their new English colony would be built at this spot. "Huzzah! Huzzah!" the group shouted. Sam and Nate danced a giddy jig of happiness.

Aboard ship that night, Sam lay on his blanket beside James. The boys talked quietly about Virginia, their new home. Long after the men had fallen asleep, the boys lay awake, too excited to sleep.

"Remember those rhymes we used to invent?" James asked. "I've just thought of a new line. 'We crossed the waves to find a world new. A hundred settlers, not just a few. The sky was our church, the ship was our pew.'" Then he added: "We weathered storms on the ocean blue." James sighed. "Now it's your turn, Sam."

The boys lay quietly on the gently swaying ship. Sam strained to think up a new line to add to the rhyme. When at last he had one, he recited the whole poem aloud: "We crossed the waves to find a world new. A hundred settlers, not just a few. The sky was our church, the ship was our pew. We weathered storms on the ocean blue. Of blessed Virginny, we at last had a view.

"Your turn, James." Sam waited for a reply. But James's quiet, even breathing told Sam that his friend had fallen fast asleep.

Sam repeated his line so he wouldn't forget it. "Of blessed Virginny, we at last had a view." Then he too fell asleep, cradled by the waters of his new home.

Life Along the James River

As soon as the place was chosen, the work began. There was so much work to do! From dawn until dark, the Englishmen unloaded supplies from the holds of all three ships and set up camp. They cut trees, trimmed off the small branches, and dragged the trunks to the riverbank. All the passengers had been idle during the crossing, and their muscles ached from the new activity. The gentlemen, especially, grumbled about having to work so hard.

Sam had no time to think about the dangers in this new world or to miss his family in England. He was so exhausted at night that he sank onto his blankets and fell asleep as soon as he shut his eyes.

One night, about a week after work on the settlement had begun, Smith crawled into their tent and woke Sam. "How would you like to go exploring?" Smith said.

Sam propped himself up on an elbow. "Exploring? Do you mean with Captain Newport?" Sam's voice trembled with excitement.

"Yes, lad," Smith answered. "I mean with Captain Newport. And about twenty others. We're going to take the shallop and look for the headwaters of our river. Meet the natives who live upstream. The captain said we'll leave tomorrow."

"Captain Newport chose you to go with him?" Sam asked, surprised. "Even though...." Sam caught himself before he finished. In the darkness, he strained to see Smith's face. He hoped his hasty words hadn't offended his master.

"Yes, Sam. Captain Newport chose me to go on his exploring trip." Smith's tone was even. "Even though he did not allow me to take my rightful place on the council. At least he appreciates my ability as an explorer." Smith began to undress.

"Will Master Calthrop be going on the exploring trip, too?" Sam asked. "And Nate? Or James?"

"No, lad. Master Calthrop will stay here at the settlement. And Master Wingfield will be in charge while Captain Newport is gone. So Nate and James will both stay here." Smith untied his breeches and stepped out of them. Wearing his shirt, which hung down to his thighs, Smith spread his blanket on the ground. "You're a lucky lad, Sam Collier," Smith said. "You're going to be the first English boy to explore Virginia."

Sam felt a tiny bit nervous about going into the wilderness with only a small group of men. *How many natives live along the river?* Sam wondered. *How will they react to us?* But he comforted himself by repeating Smith's words. "A lucky lad.... The first English boy to explore Virginia."

In the morning, Captain Newport met with Wingfield to discuss the tasks the colonists should undertake in his absence. Then he ordered his sailors to load supplies aboard the shallop.

Sam packed his and Master's Smith's belongings. At noon, the explorers pushed the shallop into the river. It was the twenty-first of May, and the settlement was far from finished. The outer walls hadn't been built. The storehouse was not ready to hold the supplies from the ships' holds. The colonists were sleeping in tents on the bare ground, rather than in permanent buildings. But the Virginia Company's instructions were clear: Captain Newport was supposed to explore the river before he returned to England. The quicker the Englishmen found gold, the quicker the company's investors would get rich.

In addition to Smith and the sailors, Captain Newport had chosen four gentlemen to take on this expedition—the writer, George Percy; Gabriel Archer, the gentleman whose hands had been injured by the Indians' arrows; and two others. On the first afternoon, the explorers traveled about eighteen miles upriver, to a point where an Indian village stood on meadowland that jutted into the river. The Indians, who called their village Weyanock, gave the Englishmen a friendly greeting.

Since the Indians and the explorers didn't know each other's languages, they communicated with their hands. They pointed at objects or made pictures in the air or dirt. Soon enough, they were exchanging simple words from each other's languages.

Using these words and pointing to scars on their bodies, the Indians explained that they were enemies of another Indian tribe. Sam counted how many Weyanock braves had scars. *They must have lots of battles,* he thought. *Now that we live in Virginia, are they going to have battles with us?*

Captain Newport put his hand on his heart and assured the Weyanocks that the Englishmen intended to be their friends. After that, the villagers danced for their visitors, just as the Kecoughtans had danced to welcome them a month ago, when their ships first sailed into Virginia.

Smith said little during the dancing. He seemed to be deep in thought. When he got up to return to the boat, Sam fell in step beside him. "Sam," Smith said, "pay close attention when we meet the natives of this land. I want you to be my second pair of eyes and ears. Memorize the words in the Indians' language.

Notice how they grow their crops, how they make their clothes, how they cook—the smallest details."

"But why—" Sam began.

Smith didn't wait for the boy's question. "I don't know how we'll use this information. But I think it will be very important. Maybe it will mean the difference between life and death in this new world."

That night, the English explorers slept in their shallop. Next morning, they got an early start and traveled some sixteen miles before the day grew very hot. Around noon, they anchored off an island where they shot enough wild turkeys and blackbirds for a hearty noonday meal. While they were roasting the fowl, a canoe holding eight Indians approached the island.

The explorers called out a greeting, using a word the Weyanock had taught them. "*Wingapoh!*" they shouted, "Friend! *Wingapoh!* Good man!"

The Indians pulled their canoe ashore, and Newport stepped forward. "How far does this river go?" he asked, sweeping his arm out toward the river's source. "Where does this water come from?"

The Indians looked puzzled. Newport tried again, but he wasn't able to make himself understood. John Smith was standing beside him, and Newport turned to him. "Can you get them to tell us what we'll find upstream?"

Smith pointed upstream. "What is up there?" he asked. Then he knelt to touch the river's surface as he said the word, "river." He made little scallops with his hand as if it was a boat riding up the river.

One of the Indians squatted beside Smith and imitated the sound of the English word, "river."

Smith smiled and nodded. "Yes. River." He drew two parallel lines in the sand and repeated the word, "river."

Smith made a circle inside the parallel lines and pointed to it, saying, "Here. Island." Then he stood up and stamped on the ground, repeating the word. "Island. You and I are here, on this island."

The Indian nodded and repeated, "island."

Smith moved back to the edge of the river and made his hand ride up and down toward the river's source. "Where does the river come from?"

The Indian grunted and began to draw a map in the sand. Before he left, this Indian gestured to show that he could bring food to trade if the explorers were interested. Smith nodded.

Sam paid close attention to this exchange. *I understood everything that Indian told my master!* he thought, pleased with himself.

The explorers continued up the river another six miles. There they found the same Indian standing on the riverbank, waving. Beside him were two women and another man, each holding baskets. Captain Newport ordered the sailors to pull the shallop to the bank so he could barter with them. In exchange for the baskets of dried oysters, mulberries, nuts, and corn, Newport offered small knives, shiny bells, and other metal trinkets.

When night fell on the second day of the expedition, the shallop had traveled another forty miles up the river.

The next morning, Sam spotted the same Indian trader on the riverbank. "There he is again!" Sam called. "That Indian who drew a map for us!"

The Indian gestured for the explorers to go with him. Captain Newport ordered two sailors to guard the boat and took the others with him. They followed the Indian to a nearby village.

As they neared the village, Sam saw twenty or thirty rounded dwellings covered with woven reeds. In an open area in the center of these houses, a group of Indian men stood around mats spread in a square on the ground. A man sitting on one of the mats—Sam guessed he was the village chief—gestured for Captain Newport to sit facing him. The chief touched his chest and said his name, Arahatec. He motioned for the other Englishmen to sit. Sam sat beside John Smith.

Women were crouching by fires, cooking little cakes of corn that smelled delicious. As soon as Sam and the others were seated, some of the women served wooden bowls of cakes, mulberries, and beans. Munching, Sam smiled at a group of small, naked children who huddled by the reed homes and stared at him.

Arahatec presented a gift to Captain Newport. It was a circlet of deer's fur, dyed bright red, meant to be worn on the head. Captain Newport beamed as he took off his iron helmet and replaced it with his new fur piece. In return, Newport gave Arahatec some small metal tools.

Two Indians carried over a large roasted deer. The women carved it into pieces and heated the pieces over the flames before serving generous helpings.

"Were these villagers expecting us?" Sam whispered. He wiped the oily meat juice off his chin with his sleeve. "They've made us a feast!"

Smith nodded. "I think so, Sam. My guess is that our trader is stopping at the villages along the river to tell the Indians about our arrival. He seems to be spreading good words about us, because these people are very hospitable."

As they talked and feasted, the Englishmen learned that Arahatec's village, like Weyanock and most of the other villages upstream, was part of the Powhatan empire. Although Arahatec was the chief of his village, he took orders from a higher ruler, a great leader called Powhatan.

Suddenly, a messenger came running into the circle, spoke rapidly to Arahatec, then ran back the way he came. Through gestures, Arahatec explained that another chief was about to arrive.

Sam looked at Smith, who had put down his food and reached for his gun.

All the Indian braves except Arahatec formed a human fence around the cluster of mats where the Englishmen sat. The sailors looked at each other nervously.

As the other chief and his warriors entered the circle, the villagers saluted him with a long shout. The chief introduced himself as Parahunt. By signs, Arahatec explained that Parahunt was the son of the Indian emperor Powhatan.

Captain Newport gave Parahunt gifts—little knives and shears made of iron, tinkling bells, and bright glass beads. Sam knew that on the streets of England, the knives were known as "penny knives," and the other gifts would be considered mere trinkets or toys. But Parahunt seemed pleased with them. He announced that he would send messengers to other villages upriver to spread the word about the arrival of the Englishmen. That way, the explorers would receive food and welcome at each stop. He also ordered five of his warriors to accompany the Englishmen as guides.

After the feast, the explorers followed their Indian guides to the river, boarded the shallop, and pushed off. As they traveled, they conversed with their hands. The Englishmen had all sorts of questions about the river, the countryside, and what the Indians grew and ate. Even though several exchanges were going on at the same time, Sam tried to pay attention to all of them.

Ten miles up the river, the boat reached an island where another village was located. The Indian guides gestured for the sailors to drop anchor. Then they led the explorers through a cultivated plain. The Englishmen marveled at the carefully tended fields and the thriving crops. Even Sam could tell that the soil was remarkably fertile. He recognized rows of beans and peas, but he had never seen corn, gourds, or tobacco growing in the fields back home. The explorers followed their guides up a hill, where Arahatec and Parahunt sat waiting on mats. Arahatec

A man sat on one of the mats—
Sam guessed it was the village chief.

invited the explorers to sit, and again women served food—mulberries and strawberries.

Then Arahatec stood and made a speech. He waved his arm to indicate the land in all directions and said that all that land belonged to Powhatan's empire. Looking at Captain Newport, Arahatec invited the Englishmen to be part of this empire. Newport nodded in agreement, and the Indian chiefs seemed delighted. Arahatec removed his own deerskin robe and placed it on Newport's back. With his hand over his heart, Arahatec declared, "*Wingapoh chemuze.*"

Captain Newport stood up. "Again, we thank you for your hospitality," he said. "And we are proud to be the allies of such a mighty and prosperous empire. Now we wish to return to the river. We have much to see of this beautiful country."

Arahatec sent six Indians to guide the explorers. To demonstrate friendship and trust, Captain Newport ordered Robert Markham, one of the sailors, to remain with the chiefs. As soon as Markham sat down, an Indian woman brought him a bowl of corn cakes.

Markham grinned and waved as the other sailors left the village. "Now don't you worry about me, fellows," he called. "I'm going to sit right here and help these Indian ladies get rid of some of this extra food. Don't want it spoiling in this heat, you know!"

Sam chuckled as he followed Smith to the shallop. The explorers found the next three miles slow going. The sailors had to maneuver the boat through rapids and avoid rocks jutting out of the river. When they reached a small waterfall that tumbled from a side stream into the river, the captain ordered the sailors to drop anchor for the night.

Five of the Indian guides got out of the boat. Captain Newport said, "The sailor," and he pointed at one of his men.

"The sailor who stayed at the village—Robert Markham. Bring him back to us."

The Indians nodded and turned to leave. The sixth Indian motioned that he'd like to remain. While they waited for Markham, this Indian said that his name was Nauirans and that he was brother-in-law to Chief Arahatec. Sam listened intently as Nauirans spoke. Once Nauirans looked over and smiled pleasantly at Sam.

Soon Markham arrived, full of stories of the kindness and hospitality he had received. "The Indian ladies laid mats under a tree so I could rest myself in the shade," he said. "And they brought me bowls of fruit and nuts. By God, they doted on me like I was a prince come home from the Crusades! Next time you need a fellow to stay with them Indians, just you ask me, Cap'n."

That night, Sam had many questions for his master. "The natives who live here in Virginia have villages and farmlands and kings. Are you surprised to learn that they join together with other villages to make empires?" he asked. "To learn that they have one great leader as well as village chiefs? And that they have wars with other Indians?"

"I am surprised, Sam," Smith admitted. "I've learned a great deal about the people who live in Virginia. And I suspect," he added, "that there's a great deal left to learn."

On Sunday morning, Newport decided he should return the hospitality of their new Indian allies. He sent a messenger to invite Chief Arahatec and King Parahunt to dinner. Newport ordered the sailors to prepare a meal of smoked pork.

In a few hours, the chiefs arrived, followed by a band of their men. The Indians milled about, watching the sailors cook and examining the Englishmen's gear. As the chiefs talked with Captain Newport and the English gentlemen, Sam edged close to Smith so he could hear.

Arahatec shook his head to indicate that he did not plan to stay and eat with the Englishmen. But he invited the explorers to return to his village when they were heading home from their expedition.

Just then, one of the sailors called out, "Cap'n, we're missing two bullet bags! They were on top of our gear when we started cooking, and now they're gone."

Sam gasped. In England, theft was often punished by death. And the theft of ammunition was especially grave.

Captain Newport's face instantly turned stormy. Quickly, John Smith stepped forward and made signs to explain the problem to the Indian leaders.

Arahatec barked a command at his men, who replied in hurried words. One Indian produced two empty pouches and placed them in Newport's hands. Then he collected the shot and small items that had been inside the bag. Another man stepped forward and returned a knife, which the sailors had not even noticed was missing.

When all the stolen goods had been returned, Captain Newport told the Indian leaders that the English looked upon theft as a very serious crime. "But," he added, "because your warriors do not understand how bad their crime was, we will forgive them. If your men wish to take home souvenirs of our visit, I will give them these as gifts." Keeping the ammunition, he handed the bags and other small items back to the Indians.

Sam sighed, relieved. But he wondered, *Do the Indians think it's all right to take an object that is left out in the open? Perhaps they have different notions of crime than we do.* Sam mulled this over. He'd never thought about what made an action right or wrong—he'd always just accepted what his parents had told him.

Who decides what a crime is? Sam asked himself. *The Indians may consider some of our actions to be crimes. Would they punish us, even if we didn't know we did something bad?* The more Sam puzzled over these questions, the more confused he felt. Finally, he brushed them aside and busied himself gathering dry wood to build up the cooking fires.

Arahatec left, taking some of his men with him, but Parahunt and the other Indians remained for the meal. Sailors had hung the boat's sail between two trees, and Captain Newport invited Parahunt to sit with him under its shade. Parahunt ate a large serving of pork and eagerly tasted the beer that the captain offered him.

Parahunt and the other Indians left after dinner, but Nauirans boarded the boat with the explorers. The sailors guided the shallop upstream through the rippling waters. Soon the river began to flow swiftly between boulders and around small islands. Newport ordered the sailors to pull the boat up at an island.

"I have decided that we will go no farther on our present expedition," Newport announced. "On this spot, I erect a cross. I hereby claim this river for England!"

Newport pounded a wooden cross into the soil. On the wood was the Latin name of England's King James, "Jacobus Rex," as well as the date, "1607." With his knife, Newport carved his own name below the king's, because he was the leader of the expedition that discovered this river and named it for his sovereign.

"I name this mighty river for the glory of England!" Newport declared grandly as he straightened up and faced his men. "Henceforth, it will be known as King James's River. The River James."

"Huzzah!" all of the explorers shouted. "For the glory of King James! Huzzah!"

Nauirans frowned as the men shouted. He moved forward. Gesturing with his hands, he asked the meaning of the captain's words and the shouting.

Newport smiled and pointed to the vertical stick on the cross. "This is King Powhatan, tall and mighty," Newport lied. Pointing to the horizontal stick, he added, "And this is Captain

Newport, the head of the English settlement. Where our sticks are fastened together in the middle, we are one. United." Newport swept his arm around the group. "My men shouted to show their respect for our alliance. They are proud to be friends of the Powhatans."

Nauirans nodded, pleased. He glanced at Sam and smiled. Ashamed of the lie that Newport had told, Sam avoided meeting Nauirans's eyes.

Then the Englishmen scrambled among the rocks, exploring the area. They walked upstream along the riverbank until they came to a waterfall. Nauirans told them it would take many days to walk to the spot where two small streams flow together to create this mighty river.

After a few hours, Captain Newport gestured for Nauirans to find Parahunt and bring him to the falls. When Nauirans returned with his king, Newport waded ashore and presented a fine hatchet to Parahunt. Nauirans encouraged the explorers to stand on the deck of the shallop and cheer. The Englishmen made a great show of enthusiasm. "Huzzah for Parahunt!" they shouted. "Farewell, King of the Powhatans! Good-bye, our Indian ally! *Wingapoh!*"

Sam shouted, too. But he felt guilty, thinking of their shout at the planting of the cross on the little island. *Captain Newport lied to Nauirans,* he thought. *Parahunt would be angry if he knew that we claimed this river for our King James. Maybe the Indians have different ideas about right and wrong, but in England I was taught that lying is a sin.*

Parahunt and his men took off their capes and waved them above their heads as they shouted a return farewell. Then Captain Newport stepped into the shallop, and the sailors, who had been holding the boat in place with their oars, let it drift down the river with the current. They ran up the sail, and the shallop picked up speed.

The expedition reached Arahatec's village after nightfall. They found that the villagers had prepared a meal to welcome back their English friends.

The next day, the explorers toured the Indian homes and fields. Sam wandered among the cooking fires and smelled roasting meat and hearty stews. Curious children pulled at his clothing and touched his skin.

Sam studied the Indian women as they worked. They wore very little clothing, and he was amazed by their nakedness. Back in England, women wore dresses that covered them from chest to toe, even in hot weather. When Sam's mother and grandmother worked, they tucked their hair under white caps. But the Indian women let their black hair hang in loose clumps on their shoulders. The Indian girls around Sam's age wore their hair shaved, except for a long braid hanging down in back.

One of the village women smiled at Sam and offered him a chunk of warm bread made from ground corn. As he bit into it, Sam thought of the kitchen at his family's farm. His mother used to hand him little bits of food to tide him over until dinner. Suddenly, he wished he was back home in England. He longed to be surrounded by familiar things, to smell English food cooking over hearth fires, to see his family, and to understand all the words that people spoke.

Thoughts of England disappeared in the afternoon when Sam watched the Indians demonstrate how they fought, using trees as shields. His eyes lit up as the Indians jabbed the air with wooden swords to show how they attacked their enemies.

In return, Captain Newport ordered Smith to demonstrate an English gun. When Smith fired the gun, the noise startled the villagers, who clamped their hands over their ears. Sam chuckled when a few frightened Indians jumped into the river.

Smiling, Smith announced, "The noise will not harm you."

He rested his gun on the ground and put his hand on his heart. "We are your friends," he gestured. "We use our guns only against enemies."

Cautiously, the Indians approached. They reached out their hands and gingerly touched the metal gun barrel.

Next day, the explorers continued downstream until they reached Point Weyanock, where they made camp. In the morning, Nauirans directed some villagers to catch fish and bring baskets full of them to the Englishmen. Then he called Sam, lifted the boy's chin, and looked into his eyes and said something. Sam narrowed his eyes, trying to understand. But before he could ask Nauirans to explain, the man turned to Captain Newport and announced that he was leaving.

Captain Newport was startled. "You're leaving? I expected you'd stay with us until we got back to our settlement, Nauirans," said the captain. "Your presence has assured us of safe passage through your people's villages. You've guided us and shown us your customs. I want to take you to the fort we're building and show you our English customs."

Nauirans smiled. He said something and held up three, then four fingers.

"So you'll stay with us?" asked Newport.

Nauirans turned and walked briskly into the forest.

Smith said, "I wonder why he was in such a hurry to leave? I thought he'd taken a liking to us."

"He held up four fingers. Maybe he meant he'd return in that amount of time," Sam suggested. "Perhaps he'll come to our settlement in four days."

Newport rubbed his chin with his hand. "Something doesn't make sense. Why would our Indian guide walk off so abruptly? With no explanation?"

The men began to mutter. Captain Newport's eyes scanned

the river as if he was expecting visitors. Smith picked up his gun and walked the length of their camp, peering into the shadows between the trees.

"What's the matter? What are the men saying?" Sam asked.

"They're afraid the Indians have betrayed us, Sam. Captain Newport thinks we'd better cut our expedition short and return to the settlement today."

Every muscle in Sam's body tightened. *Are we going to be attacked?* He remembered the battle scars on the Weyanock men. *Did we understand what the Indians said to us? Perhaps it was not friendship they were offering.*

Danger Every Minute

As soon as he caught sight of the settlement, Sam could tell something was wrong. There was no activity on the riverbank and no sound of trees being felled in the nearby forest. Around the tents, men stood guard.

Leaving a couple of sailors to secure the shallop, Captain Newport hurried up the bank. Sam and the others followed. The guards greeted them with tense, frightened faces.

"We were ambushed yesterday, Cap'n. Seventeen wounded," a guard related. "And one dead—a boy."

The color drained out of Sam's face. "Nate?" he asked.

The guard tilted his head toward Calthrop's tent, and Sam scrambled inside.

Calthrop and nine other men were huddled inside the tent. They looked up when Sam pushed his way in. He scanned their faces, searching frantically for Nate.

"Sam Collier!" said a familiar voice.

Sam gave a sigh of relief and crawled over to Nate.

Nate peered at him in the dim light. "You're back! Thank God you're safe and sound, Sam! After they ambushed us, we feared the savages might attack the shallop, too."

"The guard told me a boy was killed!" Sam said. "I was afraid...."

"You can't imagine how horrible it was, Sam." Nate's voice began to tremble. "The savages crept up on us, surrounded the fort. There must have been two hundred of them. All of a sudden, they began shrieking. Arrows were flying everywhere! Men were screaming! Most of our guns were still packed in crates. We couldn't defend ourselves, and we had no place to hide."

"Is it true that a boy was killed? Who? Richard Mutton?" Sam paused. "Not James?"

Nate looked away.

"James!" Sam cried. "James Brumfield? He's dead?"

Silence. Sam thought he saw tears on Nate's cheeks.

Calthrop leaned over and put his hand on Sam's shoulder. "It's true, Sam. James is dead. He must have made a dash for the *Discovery* during the attack. It happened so fast," Calthrop said. "So many men were wounded and bleeding. After the savages finally ran off, Master Edward called the boy, but he didn't answer. Nobody knew where he was."

"I climbed aboard the *Discovery* looking for cloth for bandages," Nate said. "That's when I found him. He was curled on his side. He didn't answer when I called to him, but his eyes were open."

Nate's voice broke. "You remember how scared he always was? Of the ocean, of the natives, of everything? I bent down and rolled him over. That's when I saw the arrow in his neck. Oh, Sam, he was dead as a stone! The Indians killed him! They killed James!"

Sam was stunned. "They killed James," he repeated softly, trying to make himself believe the news. *When did I last see him?* Sam asked himself. *I forgot to go find him before I went aboard the shallop. I didn't say good-bye.*

Sam remembered crouching beside James, on the night their ship pitched and heaved in that terrible storm. He remembered telling James they'd ride out the storm. That everything would be fine. *Little, nervous James,* Sam thought. *He'll never get seasick again. He'll never get used to Virginia or see England again. He'll never become a man.*

⁓

Fearing the Indians might attack again, the settlers did not take the time to make a casket for James. After all, he was only a child. Two sailors wrapped his little body in an old cloth and laid it in the damp ground.

During the funeral service, Sam stood between Master Smith and Nate. Memories of James flooded Sam's mind and drove out all other thoughts. Reverend Hunt led the colony in a psalm. Sam was aware of the minister's voice, but it was sound without meaning for him.

Sam remembered how he had snatched off James's cap when the fleet was docked at Blackwall Port. He remembered how irritated he was when James kept chattering about sea serpents and giant crabs on the morning the ships left the Canary Islands. *I wish I hadn't snapped at him,* Sam thought miserably.

In his mind, he saw James's nimble hands grabbing the little birds on Monito. He could almost hear James's voice, calling an alligator a "loathsome beast." That thought made Sam smile a little. He remembered lying on his blanket beside James on the night the colonists chose this site for their settlement, and how James had excitedly told him the new line he had made up for one of their shipboard poems. Silently, Sam recited their verse:

We crossed the waves to find a world new,
A hundred settlers, not just a few.
The sky was our church, the ship was our pew,
We weathered storms on the ocean blue.
Of blessed Virginny, we at last had a view.

Suddenly, Sam realized that he hadn't told James the last line of the poem. *James fell asleep before I had a chance to tell him. If only I'd told him the new line I made up!* he thought. One hot tear inched down Sam's cheek as he watched the sailors shovel clumps of dirt into his friend's shallow grave. *Of blessed Virginny, we at last had a view.* Over and over, he repeated the line, wishing James could hear it before the earth covered his ears. "Of blessed Virginny, you had a brief view," Sam whispered. Finally, he added one last line: *To our dream of a new world, you died holding true.* Sam knew the poem was finished now. It had become the epitaph for his little friend.

During the rest of the day, all the talk inside the fort was about the ambush. Sam heard the details again and again. By evening, Sam could imagine the attack so vividly that he almost felt as if he'd been there. He knew the settlers had lost precious minutes trying to unpack weapons and ammunition while the Indians' arrows rained down on them.

Sam listened as Calthrop described the attack to Smith. Four of the council members had been wounded while defending the fort. Master Wingfield had led the English defense, and he had narrowly escaped death when an arrow flew right through his beard.

During the ambush, some of the men made a desperate dash for the ships. When they reached the *Susan Constant,* they fired its cannon. All the settlers agreed that's what saved the day.

"We were fortunate," Calthrop said. "When we fired the cannon, the noise startled the Indians. Then the cannonball slammed into the trees and knocked down a heavy branch. The branch made a great racket when it landed on some of the Indians. That started the whole lot of savages howling and running off, like they'd been attacked by magical forces."

"We won't be so fortunate next time," Smith remarked. "It won't take the Indians long to realize that our cannon simply knocked down a branch. The Indians are brave fighters. When we were in their villages, some of them showed us their battle scars. They're not afraid of hand-to-hand combat."

"You went into the savages' village?" Calthrop asked him, astounded.

"We went into village after village. They showed us the fields where they plant their crops. The houses where they live. How they hunt and fish. Even how they do battle. The Indians offered us great hospitality, Stephen. They feasted us and supplied us with guides for our journey."

"Monsters! Treacherous monsters!" hissed Calthrop. "While they kept you busy feasting, they sneaked up on our settlement to massacre the rest of us!"

"I don't know," said Smith, thoughtfully. "I don't know if Parahunt's people betrayed us."

"John, what are you talking about? The Indians ambushed us! We were unarmed. They tried to wipe out every man of us. If that isn't betrayal, I don't know what is!"

"There are different groups of Indians, Stephen. Almost like the nations in Europe," Smith explained. "They have wars with each other. On our expedition, we met the Indians who are ruled by Powhatan. Perhaps another group of—"

Calthrop didn't wait to hear the rest of Smith's explanation. He shook his head and stomped off.

~

Sam was back at the settlement only two days before a group of Indians attacked again, on Friday, May 29. This time, the Englishmen were ready. They fired, but the Indians kept out of range of the guns. Many arrows landed around the tents, but the Indians were too far away from the fort to aim accurately, and no Englishmen were hurt. The colonists dared not leave the guarded area the rest of that day, even though they had so much work to do.

The next day was calm, and the Englishmen cautiously returned to the woods to fell trees. But the following day, when a colonist named Eustace Clovell left the fort unarmed, he was attacked by Indians hiding in the thickets. Clovell staggered back to the fort screaming, "Arm! Arm yourselves!" He had six arrows sticking out of him.

While the men frantically grabbed their guns, Sam and Nate ran to help carry the wounded man into a tent. One of the colony's two surgeons gave him a swig of liquor and told him to bite down on a strip of leather. The boys held down Clovell's arms while the surgeon pulled out the arrowheads, one by one, and Clovell writhed with pain. Beads of sweat dotted his face, and muffled screams came from between his clenched teeth. The surgeon stuffed cloth into Clovell's wounds to stop him from bleeding to death. But Clovell's blood seeped through the cloth and formed dark puddles on the blanket underneath him.

After removing the arrows, the surgeon told Sam and Nate to bathe Clovell's forehead with cool water until he fell asleep.

Sam looked at Nate. *Are you as scared as I am?* he wanted to ask. *If the Indians keep attacking, we'll all be killed!* Sam wished he could run away from this place of death, where they were surrounded by danger every minute. His stomach was churning with fear, and he forgot all about his vow to bravely face whatever happened in Virginia.

The next day, the first of June, Indians attacked again. This time, twenty braves knelt in the thicket and shot arrows at the fort, but the settlers' gunfire kept them from advancing close enough to injure anybody.

All was peaceful during the next two days, and the colonists cautiously resumed work. Captain Newport would soon be sailing back to England so the settlers had to hurry and cut down trees to fill the hold with clapboard that could be sold as wallboards and shingles. Meanwhile, other colonists sowed a field with wheat, and the sailors dug up sassafras roots for sale in England.

Sam and Nate were assigned to trim the branches off tree trunks. The weather continued hot and humid, and the boys had to mop their foreheads with their sleeves to keep the sweat out of their eyes. Even in the late afternoons, when the sun dipped behind the tall trees, it was uncomfortably warm. Mosquitoes took advantage of any shade and buzzed around Sam's sweaty eyes. Mayflies stung his neck and arms.

While they worked, Sam kept alert for strange noises. All the colonists expected the Indians to attack again. They just didn't know when it would happen.

For the next few days the colonists saw no signs of Indians, and they made great progress with their work. Some of the men thought the Indians were so afraid of the English guns and cannons that they had given up, but Newport continued to post guards wherever the men were at work.

Sam hoped there was another reason for the calm. He hoped the Indians they'd met on their expedition—their allies—had come to the defense of the colony. *If Nauirans and our other Indian friends have heard of the attacks, they'd organize a war party to defend us.* Although these thoughts comforted him, Sam didn't voice them. He was not nearly as confident of the Indians' friendship as he wished he was.

Several days later, Eustace Clovell died from his wounds. After he was buried, the colonists quietly resumed work. Each man prayed that Clovell would be the last of their number to die at the hands of the natives, but most of the settlers suspected that Indian attacks were going to be a constant threat in Virginia.

In the afternoon, the colonist on guard duty in the woods spotted five Indians in the distance. Two of them seemed to be unarmed, and they shouted, "*Wingapoh!*" The other three carried bows and arrows. The guard shot at the Indians, and they ran away.

"The guard shot at them?" cried Sam when he heard about the incident. "Those Indians were our allies! They were saying '*Wingapoh*' to show they were our friends!"

"Be reasonable, Sam. The guard wasn't on your expedition," Nate said. "How was he supposed to know that those Indians were our allies? Besides, how do you know they were really friends? Maybe it was a trick. The savages have crouched in the bushes waiting to attack when we leave the fort. They've even hidden below the walls of our fort and shot at unarmed men wishing only to relieve themselves! How can we trust any of the Indians?"

Sam didn't know what to answer. But he thought about their friendly Indian guide, Nauirans, who had smiled at him when they were aboard the shallop. He remembered the gentle woman who offered him bread. Then he pictured Eustace Clovell, writhing with pain as the surgeon pulled the arrows out of his bloody body. Sam shuddered at the thought of little James Brumfield, lying dead with an arrow sticking out of his neck.

~

The *Susan Constant* and *Godspeed* were almost packed to return to England. The smallest ship, the *Discovery*, would be staying at Jamestown. On June 10, Captain Newport met with the council to resolve various complaints about conditions in the settlement. During the meeting, Reverend Hunt requested that John Smith be placed on the council.

"That was the expressed instruction of the Virginia Company, gentlemen," Hunt said. "Now that we've reached Virginia, I think the wisdom of the company's directors is evident. John Smith has demonstrated that he is both an able and a resourceful leader."

None of the settlers, not even Master Wingfield, argued.

Newport thanked Hunt for bringing up the matter. He praised Smith's behavior during their exploration. "Smith is the type of man who can be depended upon in the wilderness," Newport said. "I'm convinced that the council will benefit from his opinion. The man learned how to deal with heathens in Turkey, you know, and he has a knack for communicating with natives."

Sam was as delighted as his master about the council's decision. *At last,* he thought, *the men have come to their senses and put aside hard feelings from the voyage.*

For a few days, work at the fort continued peacefully. But on June 13, two Englishmen were ambushed by eight Indians hiding in the long grasses. One of the colonists was seriously injured by an arrow that lodged in his chest. This new incident reminded everyone to be watchful.

The next day, Sam and Nate were sent to help cut trees for clapboard. At noontime, they wandered away from the men to search for wild strawberries. As they stooped to gather the fruit, Sam spotted two brown-skinned men walking through the trees. "Look, Nate!" he cried. "Indians!"

Nate's face turned white, and the boys looked around frantically for cover.

They were about to run to the settlement when Sam recognized one of the Indians. He waved and shouted, "*Wingapoh!*"

The Indian waved back and called several words in greeting.

"That's the Indian who traded with us, Nate!" Sam said. He approached the men, but Nate stood back, watching.

Sam told the Indians about the attacks on the fort. Turning to Nate, he said, "Go get Captain Newport. If we bring these men any closer to the fort, the guard may panic and shoot."

Nate soon returned with Newport and Master Wingfield. "Welcome. *Wingapoh!* Ally." Newport said to the Indians. He pointed at Wingfield. "This man is a chief of our people," he said. "His name is Master Wingfield."

They exchanged greetings, and Newport repeated Sam's story about the attacks against the colonists. The Indians listened with serious expressions on their faces. The trader clasped his left arm with his right hand to show that the Indians would come to the support of their friends. He promised to speak to Chiefs Arahatec and Parahunt.

Then the Indian trader knelt and swung his hand as if to cut the long grass.

"Cut?" asked Master Wingfield, trying to understand the Indian's meaning. "Cut down the tall plants. Yes, of course!" Wingfield looked at Newport. "Do you understand what this fellow is saying, Captain? He's telling us to mow down the high grass around our fort so the wicked savages will have no place to hide. An excellent suggestion!"

Wingfield beamed and nodded his agreement. "Thank you, my good fellow." he said. "I'll have the men get right on it." He shook his head and chuckled. "Cut the grass—clever idea! It's a wonder none of us thought of it ourselves."

Word of the visit from the friendly Indians spread quickly among the colonists. Early the next morning, Newport sent Sam and Nate, Richard Mutton, and a group of sailors to cut down the high weeds and shrubs blocking the colonists' view of the area surrounding their tents.

The boys were assigned to clear a swath of ground north of the tents. It was a sticky morning, and the hot sun promised to burn through the mist.

"Nate and I will start on this side, Richard," Sam said, motioning for Nate to follow him.

"As you like. It's all the same to me." Richard shrugged and moved away.

Sam and Nate took up the scythes and cut away the tall grass near a thicket of trees and shrubs. By midmorning, the sun was beating down on Richard, but Sam and Nate were under the shade of the trees. Richard's face turned bright red, and he had to stop every few minutes to mop his forehead with his sleeve.

"Curse the savages!" he muttered. He straightened up and squinted at Sam and Nate. "Cut down the weeds, indeed! We may as well cut down the clouds for all the good it's going to do. The whole place is weeds!" Richard threw his scythe onto the ground. "If it was up to me, we'd cut down the savages, not the weeds," he grumbled. "We'll break our backs cutting these weeds, and we'll be too exhausted to fight. This is just more treachery. For all we know, those braves are planning to come back and ambush us. They may be hiding in the trees, right now, aiming their bows and arrows at us!"

Sam stood up. "Keep quiet, Richard," he said. "Those Indians are our allies. They're going to carry word to their leaders and help us defend our settlement. I met one of them—the trader—when Master Smith and I went with Captain Newport to explore the river."

Sam couldn't help gloating as he told Richard about the Indian trader. "If your master had been chosen to go on the expedition, then you would understand that the Indian trader is our friend. He brought bushels of food to barter with us. He told all the villages along the river about us. His people even came and guided our boat."

"I heard about how they guided you," Richard sneered. "They guided you away from the fort, so they could ambush us when our numbers were low. If your master had a lick of sense, he would have noticed how the savages kept delaying you. How they wouldn't let you come back down the river to the settlement. Friends—hah! They're murderers. Bloodthirsty wolves!"

Sam balled his hands into fists and ran at Richard, but the larger boy pushed him off and heaved him onto the ground.

"Stop!" Nate shouted. "Stop fighting! The captain sent us out here to clear the weeds, not argue." Nate came up behind Sam, grabbed his shoulders, and dragged him out from under Richard's big fists.

Sam jerked around and yelled at Nate, "You heard him say Master Smith has no sense. He called our allies bloodthirsty wolves!"

"I heard him, Sam," Nate said, pulling his friend by the arm. "Richard has a big mouth. But we have work to do."

"Nate, you don't believe what he's saying?" Sam protested. "Do you?"

"Perhaps I do, perhaps I don't know what to believe," Nate said. "Indians have attacked us again and again, Sam. You've seen them with your own eyes. Didn't they kill James Brumfield? Didn't they kill Eustace Clovell?"

"Are you saying that Master Smith hasn't any sense?" Sam demanded.

"I'm saying that the Indians told us to cut down the weeds, and I think that's a good idea. So that's what I'm going to do." Nate paused. "I'm also saying we don't know enough about Indians to judge whether they're friends or enemies. Any of them—even that trader fellow." He picked up his scythe and swung it hard through the weeds.

The boys worked in angry silence the rest of the day.

⁓

On June 16, all three boys were assigned to make clapboards by splitting up tree trunks. They worked at the riverbank so the finished clapboard could be loaded easily onto the *Susan Constant* and the *Godspeed*. In late morning, an Indian canoe crossed the broad river, heading toward them. The guards began to shout, and Captain Newport ran to the edge of the water.

"*Wingapoh!*" the braves called and waved from their canoe. "*Wingapoh!*"

Captain Newport waved back at the Indians and answered, "*Wingapoh!*"

"Want me to fire above their heads to keep them out of arrow range, Cap'n?" asked the guard. "I don't trust them savages coming close to the fort."

"No, don't fire," Newport said. "I'll get into the shallop and meet them on the river."

Newport hastily ordered some of the sailors to row him out to the Indians. Sam, Nate, and Richard joined the men on the shore. Although they were too far away to hear Newport's words, they saw him gesturing. After a short conversation, the sailors raised their guns and pointed them at the Indians. The Indians quickly paddled back across the river, jeering and laughing.

When the shallop returned, Newport was fuming. "It was a trick!" he shouted. "They took me for a fool! Those savages were masquerading as our friends. Tried to get me to bring the shallop around the point, where it couldn't be seen from the fort. Said their king wanted to meet with me. But the water is too shallow for a boat out there. When I accused the scoundrels of lying, they started to laugh."

Richard edged close to Sam and said in a low voice, "Another visit from your friends, huh, Collier? Why don't you go tell Master Smith to come down here and trade with those friendly Indians, since he knows so much about them from your expedition?"

Sam wheeled around, and Richard smirked.

"I never said we should trust every Indian." Sam spat out his words between clenched teeth.

Richard ignored him and walked off.

I never said we should trust every Englishman, either, Sam thought as he glared at Richard's back.

The Seasoning

The settlement was completely enclosed by the third week of June 1607. Sam felt safe inside its sturdy palisade, which was made of split tree trunks standing side by side to form rough walls. The sharpened tips of the trunks were three times as tall as a man. The palisade enclosed a triangular-shaped piece of land overlooking the James River. A raised platform stood at each corner inside the walls. On each platform, a cannon was mounted and positioned to shoot at enemy vessels, such as Spanish ships that might come up from the bay or Indian canoes coming from either direction. Since the palisade was rounded around the platforms, the shape of their fort was a triangle with a half-moon at each corner.

On the morning of June 22, Sam carried to the *Susan Constant* the letters that his master and many of the gentlemen had written. Captain Newport would have this mail delivered when he reached London. After handing over the letters, Sam said good-bye to the sailors. He picked up Molly, his favorite ship's cat, and stroked her warm fur.

"How long do you think it will take you to get to England?" Sam asked an old sailor.

The sailor shrugged. "Have to ask the wind and the waves, lad. No use predictin'."

Sam scratched the cat's chin and listened to her ragged purr. Then he handed her to the sailor. Wishing the fellow a safe trip, he climbed down to the riverbank.

Nate and the other settlers stood on the bank, watching the sailors set the sails on the *Susan Constant* and the *Godspeed*. Clapboard from Virginia's trees filled the holds of both ships. Two tons of sassafras roots, used to flavor food and make medicines, were stored in barrels aboard the ships. As soon as the ships completed the crossing and docked in London, Captain Newport would sell the cargo, and the Virginia Company would begin to earn money from its colonial venture.

Before he boarded, Captain Newport turned and faced the ninety-eight men and three boys who would remain at James Fort. "Wish me Godspeed, men! As soon as I've sold these goods in England, I'll make ready to return. Look for me to be back in twenty weeks with supplies. And I'll bring as many new settlers as I can stuff onto the 'tween deck!"

Sam carried the letters to the Susan Constant.

Most of the men watched in silence as the ships sailed down-river, but Sam and Nate shouted and whistled as they waved. As soon as the ships disappeared around a bend, Sam thought about the long ocean crossing from England to Virginia. He remembered the danger from storms and the possibility of attacks by Spaniards and pirates.

"Do you think Captain Newport really will return in twenty weeks?" he asked Nate. "A lot can happen to a ship crossing the Atlantic Ocean."

Nate shrugged. "Twenty weeks—that's five months. It'll be late November or December before he returns." Nate avoided his friend's eyes. "A lot can happen here in Virginia, too."

John Smith gave a hearty shout, "Back to work, men! When Captain Newport returns, he'll find we've built a fine settlement for Englishmen here on the James River!"

He clamped his hands on Sam's and Nate's shoulders and gave them an encouraging smile. Turning to the men, Smith declared, "These two lads are eager to make themselves rich! How about the rest of you?"

Some of the colonists answered Smith with a cheer and headed for the fort to resume work. Others stood in stony silence. These were mostly the highborn gentlemen, who huddled around George Kendall, Richard's master. Smith ignored the do-nothings. He led Sam and Nate toward the field planted with wheat. "The company didn't send us here to be farmers. But if we're going to eat while we're waiting for the first supply ship, we'll have to tend to our crop. Our seeds sprouted, but there hasn't been enough rain." Smith knelt down and picked up a handful of dry dirt. "I want you to haul water from the river and spread it carefully along each row. The soil is very dry, so take care you don't wash away the seedlings."

Sam knew how to water seeds and care for young plants because he'd worked in his family's vegetable garden in England. But in the glare of Virginia's sun, this field seemed endless. It was going to be hot, slow work hauling water from the river to moisten all this soil. By the time they managed to water the last row of seedlings in the plot, the first row would be dry again.

Sam knew it wasn't his place to question his master's orders, but he blurted out, "What about all the others? Why aren't they working, too?"

Nate shot an alarmed look at his friend. John Smith was a kind master, but everyone knew he had a quick temper. A master had every right to beat a servant who refused to do his work.

"This plot needs water, lad!" Smith snapped. "We're going to need every bit of wheat we can grow if we're going to survive until Cap'n Newport returns with a supply ship. There are some in Virginia who understand these facts. Unfortunately, there are others who need to be convinced. But the seedlings need water now. They cannot wait until every highborn gentleman is ready to cooperate!"

His tone softened. "I'm depending on you. We've come to Virginia in search of riches, and I'm convinced we'll find them— eventually. Meanwhile, we have to eat. We must grow wheat."

Ashamed of his outburst, Sam grabbed a barrel and rolled it toward the river to fill with water. Sam knew his master was right, but he couldn't help resenting the men who stood idly beside the river, complaining about Smith and the heavy work-load. And Sam couldn't help noticing that Kendall's boy was standing as idle as the gentlemen. As Sam and Nate struggled to roll the heavy barrel of water up to the field, Richard snickered at them.

For the next month, Sam and Nate worked in field and fort. There was never a shortage of work. At least two men were needed to stand guard at each corner of the fort, day and night. Trees had to be felled, dragged to the fort, and split for firewood or building material. Hunters went out daily in search of game, and other settlers fished in the river. Every day, the sun beat down. There was little rain, and the wheat grew slowly, despite constant efforts to water it. The fort's food supplies dwindled. All the pigs brought from England had been slaughtered and eaten. The chickens, which had been brought over as breeding stock, began to die off, so the colonists killed and ate them, too. Master Wingfield ordered the remaining food to be rationed. One small can of dried barley was allowed each day for every five men. Cooks soaked the barley in water from the James River and boiled it into a gruel. They added sturgeon or crab, when the colonists were lucky enough to catch them. Each man and boy got one bowlful of the gruel a day.

For drink, the settlers depended on the river, since the kegs of beer and water from island streams were long since used up. Sam thought the river water tasted terrible. It had a slightly salty flavor, but he quickly got used to that. It was the slime floating in it that disgusted him. But, like the other settlers, Sam drank a lot of the unpleasant water because the heat and the work made him constantly thirsty. He'd never experienced such hot and humid days in England, even in midsummer.

A few weeks after the ships had sailed, several colonists became ill. They clutched their bellies and groaned. They ran fevers and were unable to hold down even the little food allowed them. In spite of the heat, they lay shivering on the ground, clasping thread-bare blankets.

Another week, and more took sick. Some of the ailing men were too weak to walk outside the fort to relieve themselves, so they soiled their clothes and the ground inside the fort. When Sam passed the sick men's tents, he held his nose because the stink was so awful.

Sam and the other healthy settlers had to take over the work for those too weak to contribute. Each day, at first light, Sam and Nate were sent to tend the wheat field, to gather firewood in the thickets, or to catch fish at the river. Even though the boys had no experience with guns, they were assigned turns at guard duty.

John Smith showed the boys how to load and fire the guns. He taught them to drop a lead slug into the gun's barrel, and then pour gunpowder into a little pan behind the slug. When the boys lit the black powder, it exploded and slammed the lead slug out the gun's barrel.

Since the guards had to be ready to fire at any moment, they wore their ammunition. Each guard kept lead slugs in a bag tied to his waist, and he carried small wooden containers filled with gunpowder on a strip of leather across his shoulder. He hung a long rope, called a slow match, around his neck and kept both ends lit. When he wanted to shoot, he would touch the smoldering tip of his match to the powder in his gun. After every shot, he would have to reload.

"Lads, take care to keep this gunpowder away from your slow match," Smith said, as he adjusted the strips of leather around the boys' shoulders so their powder containers weren't touching the burning tips of their matches. "If you aren't careful, you'll blow yourselves up!"

Sam was proud to be doing a man's work, so he never complained about standing guard duty. But the guns were heavy and awkward to carry. They were also difficult to aim. On the few occasions when Sam actually practiced firing the gun, the force of the shot nearly knocked him off his feet. Sam practiced all the steps required to reload, but he still needed at least two minutes to complete the complicated process.

By late July, sickness had spread around the fort. Every day, more of the colonists and several members of the council fell ill. Captain Bartholomew Gosnold was sick, and so were John Martin and John Ratcliffe. When John Smith announced that he felt dizzy, Sam stayed close to their tent to help his master. Sam carried buckets of water from the river. He scooped up ladlefuls of water so Smith could sip. He soaked rags and laid them on Smith's feverish forehead.

Since standing guard was the most crucial of the colonists' responsibilities, Sam took both his own and his master's turns. Sometimes, Sam stood guard for a night and a day and had only twenty-four hours before he stood guard again. He returned to the tent as often as he could to care for his sick master. *In Lincolnshire, Father made me work long hours,* Sam reflected. *But then I had plenty to eat and enough time to sleep. Here in Virginia, I have to work just as hard, but I'm always hungry and always tired. The Virginia Company said this would be an easy place to get rich. But there's nothing easy about life here!*

On the sixth of August, both of the colony's surgeons were called to see one of the sick men. The man's hands and feet were swelling, and he could not swallow water. He started to spit up blood, then lost consciousness. The surgeons were not able to bring down the man's fever or awaken him. Helpless, they watched him die. The next morning, the man was buried.

When Sam heard the news, an icy jab of fear hit him. *Master Smith has to get well,* Sam thought. *Virginia is so far from Lincolnshire. What will happen to me if my master dies?* Sam tended his patient even more carefully. He trickled water down John Smith's throat every few minutes and kept the rag on his master's forehead soaked in cool water. Sam coaxed Smith to swallow a spoonful of barley gruel whenever he woke from his feverish sleep.

As more men took sick, work in the settlement became disorganized. For days at a time, nobody watered the colony's wheat field, and the plants began to shrivel up. Little progress was made in building permanent housing, even though the tents were so mildewed and tattered that they barely provided shelter. Sam knew all this work was urgent, but he couldn't leave his master alone for long. Without water, Smith could slip into death in a few hours. When Sam had to stand guard duty, he asked Nate to look after Master Smith.

On August 9, a gentleman named George Flower died. The settlers held a short funeral for Flower and buried him that day. The next day, William Brewster died of a wound received during one of the Indian attacks. Sam and Nate were assigned the hot, depressing chore of digging Brewster's grave.

To avoid the scorching sun, the boys began early in the morning. But Sam started to sweat as soon as he lifted the shovel. His head was throbbing, and the shovel felt unusually heavy.

"What's the matter?" Nate asked.

"My head is spinning," Sam said. He sat down, but his legs wouldn't stop shaking. Suddenly, Sam felt an awful cramp in his stomach. He leaned over and vomited.

Nate put his long arm around Sam's shoulders to steady him. "Oh, Sam, you've got the sickness! Come on." Holding Sam's arm, Nate led him to John Smith's tent.

Sam wanted to protest. He didn't want Nate to have to dig the grave for Brewster all by himself. But he felt so weak. As soon as his head touched the blanket, Sam fell asleep.

In the days and nights that followed, Sam dozed in the ragged tent. He lay beside Smith on a scratchy blanket spread on the dirt. Sam's head and belly ached. His arms and legs felt sore. Feverish, he tossed and turned, muttering in his sleep. Sometimes he opened his eyes under the glaring rays of the hot, merciless sun that pierced through gashes in the tent. Sometimes he woke shivering in inky black darkness. Whenever he awakened, he longed for the feel of cold water on his dry throat.

All around him, Sam heard the pitiful cries of ailing men. Their groans and the cramps in his stomach made him wish for the relief of sleep. But when he slept, he had disturbing, horrible dreams. They seemed so real that Sam had trouble deciding when his dreams stopped and real life started.

He dreamed of running through the forest behind his brother. Panting with excitement, the two boys scrambled up a tree, racing to reach the top. Finally, Sam struggled onto a short branch at the very top of the tree, and he stopped to rest.

The little branch began to tremble. It shook more violently, and Sam clasped it with both hands to keep from tumbling to the earth. He looked down, but his brother was gone. Terrified, Sam watched as Richard Mutton grabbed the branch and shook it.

"Richard, stop that!" Sam screamed. "Let go. I'll fall!"

Richard snickered as the branch rocked from side to side. "What's the use of bringing a criminal into our new colony?" he jeered. "You'll die in the New World, Samuel Collier. You'll die before you're a man!"

Laughing, Richard shook Sam's branch so hard that it ripped off the tree. The branch plunged and heaved through the air, riding the gigantic ocean swells like the *Susan Constant* during the awful storm before the fleet reached Virginia.

Sam cried and begged, but Richard sneered and backed away in his canoe, which was full of Indians. As Sam lost his grip and plunged headlong toward the water, he could hear the Indians' laughter. Sam slammed through the surface of the ocean and awoke, gasping. His throat burned from the terrible salt of the sea, and he whimpered for a taste of cool water.

His eyes closing again, Sam thrashed from side to side in the burning rays of the cruel sun. He reached up and tore at the opening of his shirt, trying to get away from the heat. Dozing at last, his hand closed around a firm stick whose point was stuck in his neck. Sam tugged at the arrow, screaming. The burning in his throat was terrible, and he knew he was going to die.

He heard Richard's voice again.

Sam edged away from him, whimpering, "Please, Richard. Please don't roll my blanket so tight around me!" He struggled to free his arms. "I don't want to be buried under Virginia's soil!"

"Wake up, Sam! It's me...Nate. Open your eyes. I've brought you some water."

Sam squinted and saw Nate kneeling over him in the tent. Confused, Sam stopped struggling and let Nate cradle his head in his arm. Nate trickled water through Sam's chapped lips.

As the blessed water bathed his throat, Sam heard the voice of John Smith beside him. His master was muttering: "Take apart the gallows! Dismantle that cursed thing before the Turks arrive. Quick, lads!"

Gently, Nate lowered Sam's head onto the blanket. He lifted John Smith's head and trickled water down the man's parched throat. "Can you eat some porridge, Sam?" Nate asked. "How about you, Master Smith?"

Sam mumbled, drifting back into a dreamless sleep. Time passed. Sam thought he heard John Smith crawling out of the tent. Maybe others came and went. Sam wasn't sure. He lost track of time and place. One day, Sam opened his eyes and watched Master Smith scoop some water out of the bucket. Sam propped himself on an elbow and sipped as Smith held the ladle.

"Are you well now, Master Smith?" Sam asked.

"I'm much recovered, Sam," Smith said gently, "and I think your fever is beginning to break. You'll feel better soon. You're a strong lad. But the sickness has taken a heavy toll among the men." Smith paused. "Master Calthrop has taken sick. That's why Nate hasn't been coming to see you, Sam. I don't know if Stephen will make it."

Sam couldn't hold himself up any longer. He flopped back down on the blanket.

"I have to go now, Sam. I'm on duty tonight." Smith shook his head. "So many are sick. We can barely find enough men to guard the fort. I'll send one of the surgeons to look in on you."

When Sam awoke again, Nate was beside him. Nate lifted Sam's head to give him a sip of water, and Sam gulped it gratefully. The gentle light of early morning filtered through holes in the tent.

Sam felt wet. He touched his shirt and ran his hand over his blanket. "Has it rained?"

"No, Sam. You're wet from sweat," Nate said. "Your fever broke during the night. You'll get strong again now."

Sam thought he heard a choking sound in Nate's voice. He looked closely at Nate's face and smiled. "Don't worry, Nate," Sam whispered. "I'm not going to die." Sam closed his eyes.

That sound again. Now Sam was sure his friend was crying.

Sam opened his eyes and squinted at Nate. "What's wrong, Nate?"

Nate's face crumpled. "I...I'll tell you later, Sam. When you're well. Not now," he stammered, fighting back tears.

"You can tell me, Nate. What happened?"

Nate wiped his nose with the back of his hand. "It's Master Calthrop. He's dead."

Sam was astonished. He thought he must be dreaming again. *Master Calthrop?* Sam vaguely remembered hearing that Calthrop was ill. *But Master Calthrop was a young gentleman. He was strong and healthy!*

Sam looked around the tent. He touched his shirt, damp and cool against his fingertips. Then he peered at his friend. Nate's shoulders heaved up and down, and he covered his face with his hands. "Oh, Nate," Sam whispered, "I'm so sorry."

"He's dead, Sam! My master is dead. I never left his side, I swear I didn't. But he died, anyway." Nate hung his head. "He'll be buried today."

Sam couldn't think of anything to say. He just watched his friend's shoulders move up and down. Nate's sobs seemed far away. Sam tried to think, but his mind kept fluttering away. He pictured James Brumfield lying beneath Virginia's soil. He wished it would rain, so the dirt above his little friend would spring to life with fresh, green plants.

Dead, a voice inside Sam's head seemed to say. *So many are dead. Now Master Calthrop is dead, too. How long until all of us are dead?* Sam looked at Nate, and a great wave of sadness swept over him. *Poor Nate! He's all alone. An orphan here in the wilderness.*

∽

After that day, Sam grew stronger. As soon as he could, he returned to his duties. But he couldn't work as hard as he used to. After an hour, he was exhausted.

Death was never far from Sam's thoughts. Hardly a day passed without another man dying in the fort. Scores of colonists were ill, groaning on filthy blankets inside the tents. Gentlemen died—a lifetime of comfort and plenty in England did not protect them against Virginia's sickness. Common workers also died—a lifetime of hard work in England, building strong muscles and calloused hands, did not protect them against these fevers.

John Smith told Sam: "This is an ordeal that we must survive to plant a new colony, Sam. Some of us will be strong enough to live through it. Think of it as our seasoning period."

Sam nodded, but he didn't really understand what Smith meant. *What does it matter?* he thought. *I'll probably die here in Virginia.*

Nate moved into the tent with Sam and Smith. Whenever Sam looked at his friend's sad, bony face, it reminded Sam of how hopeless their situation was. *It will be a miracle if anybody lives through our seasoning to greet the supply ship from England.*

Salvation

By mid-August, Sam lost count of the men who had died. The intense heat drained the energy from the survivors. Even at night, the air felt hot and sticky. Flies and mosquitoes tormented the colonists and woke them from their sleep.

The fort's food supply was almost used up, and Sam's belly grumbled constantly. Sometimes his hunger pangs hurt so much that he thought he was coming down with the sickness again. Each day, his bowl of gruel tasted more and more like warm, salty water. Sam was as hungry when he finished eating as when he began.

With so little food, each of the survivors watched his neighbor jealously to see that no man took more than his fair share. Rumors of plots and treason spread as quickly as sickness through the fort.

"I tell you, lad, some of these gents ain't what they seem," a laborer whispered to Sam over the cooking fire one evening. "They sound like proper Englishmen, and they dress like proper Englishmen. But if you could look deep into their hearts, you'd see Spaniards!"

The man raised his eyebrows to indicate that he was talking about Master George Kendall, who was walking by. The laborer leaned closer to Sam and hissed, "Watch what you say to that one. He's a spy!"

There were rumors that Spain had placed a spy among the passengers to find out everything he could about Virginia, then abandon James Fort to set up a Spanish colony. Many men swore that Kendall was this spy, and that he'd tried to persuade them to leave with him. Sam even heard a rumor that Master Kendall had made a deal with the Indians to ignore James Fort and trade with the Spaniards instead!

Sam didn't know what to believe. Kendall had urged the colonists to hang Smith for mutiny and had refused to do any work he considered beneath him. *But that doesn't make him a spy,* Sam thought. *With our food supply so low, the men are desperate. They're turning on each other and making all kinds of wild accusations.*

The council members were preoccupied with their own illness and suffering, so they were unable to calm the colonists' suspicions. Of the six, only President Wingfield and George Kendall had not been ill. John Smith had recovered from the sickness, and John Martin was feeling a little better. But John Ratcliffe was still too weak to walk. On August 22, Bartholomew Gosnold died. Since he had been the captain of the *Godspeed*, the colonists gave him a state funeral and fired the cannons in his honor. His death left the council short by one man.

One morning, Smith told Sam the council was meeting to hear some very serious business. "I expect it will take quite a while. So you and Nate should see about the wheat before the sun gets too strong. Then try to dig out some mussels or crabs."

"Serious business?" Sam asked, as he scraped caked dirt off his master's shoes.

"Very serious. Accusations that we have an agent from Spain in our colony," Smith said.

That day, the council meeting was the topic of every conversation in James Fort. Various colonists were called to tell what they knew about the Spanish spy incident. The meeting wasn't over until late in the afternoon.

Sam and Nate were working by the riverbank when a group of men came out of the fort. George Kendall was in the midst of them, his wrists bound. As Sam and Nate watched, Kendall was led to the edge of the river and marched aboard the *Discovery*. An armed guard climbed aboard after the prisoner. Richard Mutton skulked behind, his eyes on the ground.

Sam smirked—he couldn't help himself. He wanted to yell, "Who's the criminal now, Richard? Does your master still think we should hang our criminals?"

As Richard came closer, Sam noticed the boy's face. It was bright red, and he looked as if he might cry. Sam remembered how he had felt when John Smith was taken prisoner during the crossing. An ocean separated Richard from his family, and the man he served was accused of treason! Sam didn't have the heart to taunt Richard, even if the bully did deserve a taste of his own medicine.

The scorching days of August drew slowly to a close. Each morning when Sam left his tent, he saw new corpses sprawled on the ground. The dying crawled out during the night in search of relief from their misery. As soon as the sun came up, flies buzzed around their bloated bodies. The smell was even more revolting than the sight.

The living settlers were too weak and exhausted to organize proper burials. They simply dragged the new corpses to one corner of the fort to be put in shallow graves and covered hastily with dirt.

"If Captain Newport ever does return with supplies, he may not find any colonists alive to feed," Nate muttered.

Sam nodded. He noticed that Nate's clothing hung loosely on his skinny frame, as if he wore hand-me-downs from a giant. When Sam looked at his own threadbare shirt and torn pants, he knew that he looked just as pathetic as Nate—a bony body swimming in baggy rags.

~

One morning in early September, the guards opened the gate of the fort and began to shout. Sam sat up and rubbed the sleep from his eyes. He nudged Nate. The boys scrambled out of the tent and headed toward the noise.

Two baskets filled with vegetables had been left outside. The astonished guards carried them inside, cheering triumphantly. Later that morning, several Indian men approached the fort in a canoe piled high with baskets. As they paddled toward the river-bank, the braves called, "*Wingapoh!*"

The Indians carried the baskets up to the gate and waved at the guards. Then they returned to their canoe and paddled away.

Inside the fort, some of the settlers examined the food suspiciously. They didn't trust anything that came from savages. Unpacking the corn cakes, shellfish, and meat cautiously, they sniffed for unusual odors that might indicate if the food was poisoned.

Sam was too hungry to be cautious. *I'd rather die from a belly full of poisoned food than die slowly of starvation!* Many others shared his feeling, and they fell upon the loaves of Indian bread.

Breaking off a hunk and stuffing it in his mouth, Sam sat down to concentrate on eating. The smell made him wild with hunger. He wanted to gulp down his first mouthful, but he forced himself to chew slowly and thoroughly until every crumb dissolved, until he tasted every morsel of its flavor. Then he allowed himself to swallow and take another mouthful.

"If somebody offers me a basket of gold in exchange for this bread," Sam announced, his mouth stuffed full, "I'm choosing the bread!"

John Smith grinned and helped himself to some bread. He told Sam he wasn't worried about poisoned food. Why would the Indians send poisoned food to kill them when they were already dying from starvation and sickness? But this unexpected gift puzzled Smith. Like the other settlers, Smith had come to the conclusion that the Indians wanted the Englishmen to die. Even the Powhatans, who had pledged themselves the allies of the English, had ignored the colony's suffering. It didn't make sense that the Indians would suddenly decide to help.

Tempting aromas began to drift out of the cooking pots in James Fort. Vegetables simmered in broths thickened with chunks of oysters. Venison roasted over fires and dripped rich fat onto sizzling flames. The smells were so bewitching that Sam couldn't concentrate on anything else.

Before noonday, Reverend Hunt gathered the colonists who were strong enough to walk for a brief thanksgiving service. The men bowed their heads and thanked the Lord for saving them from certain death.

Hunt reminded the colonists that their salvation had come from Indians, a most unexpected source. "Indeed those very savages who attacked ye and murdered thy comrades!" he exclaimed. "During all these weeks of agony, whilst ye watched thy fellows succumb to horrible starvation and deadly sickness, the savages delivered nought but brutality to thy gates. Behold, it is from the hands of the enemy that ye now receive thy salvation! The same savages who shed thy blood hath delivered the bread of life to thy gates. From thy mortal enemies, thou taketh the seeds that enable thee to plant civilization in this wilderness."

Hunt told the colonists to pray. "For our Lord works in strange and wonderful ways. Remember that thy suffering, though it tests the very roots of thy faith, is part of a divine plan. Yea, a plan greater than thy human ability to understand."

Sam shut his eyes and tried to thank God with all his might. But his stomach whined for food. All he could think about were the aromas drifting out of the cooking pots.

After that first full meal, Sam's enthusiasm returned in a rush. He understood that many of the settlers were too sick to recover, even with the Indians' food, and he felt sorry for their misery. But Sam refused to let death and fear fill his thoughts again. "We're alive, Nate! Master Smith says that the sickness took nearly half of our men. But you and I survived our seasoning," Sam said. "We were meant to be men of this new world!"

The boys were on a mudflat beside the river, poking sticks through the weeds in search of mussels. Their bare feet squished through the warm, gooey mud.

Nate gazed at the river. "Maybe so. But some are saying there's a curse on this colony," he said. "That James Fort is a place of death."

Nate's brooding made Sam uncomfortable. He punched his friend's arm. "Look here, Nate Peacock, I'm too lucky to die," Sam said with a grin. "And you're my best friend. The way I figure it, you're not about to die, either. Because I'm too lucky to lose my best friend!"

Sam noticed a thick tree stump at the edge of the woods. He leaped over the mud, flopped down in the weeds, and planted his right elbow on the stump. He knew Nate could never resist an invitation to arm-wrestle. *I'll lose, of course,* Sam thought. *because Nate's bigger. But at least he'll stop worrying about death and curses for a few minutes.*

Nate knelt down on the other side of the stump. He grabbed Sam's hand and drove it hard against the stump. Then he grinned.

The sound of honking brought both boys to their feet. A wedge of geese flew over the distant treetops. As the flock came closer, the clatter of squawking resounded through the air.

"Look at all those geese!" Sam exclaimed. "There are enough birds up there to feed every man in James Fort for a month!"

The boys dashed through the thicket to see where the geese were going to land. Then they ran back to the fort to alert the hunters.

Fowl continued to fly in from the north in great flocks. They settled on streams and ponds near the fort. The hunters brought back fat geese, snow-white swans, and little green and brown ducks. Indians visited the fort, bringing more baskets of food—corn on the cob, beans, squash, and corn cakes. With a greatly improved diet, the colonists' strength began to return.

But Nate was not the only colonist who had lost his taste for Virginia. Around every campfire, Sam heard grumbling and complaining. "James Fort is a cursed place," they said. "Its waters carry sickness and death." Some of the men said the Indians had cast a spell on the land and river. "Do you see how their villagers prosper? Why don't they fall ill with the sickness?"

"Nonsense!" Smith spat. "The Indians prosper because they work the land and fish the river—not because they cast spells."

All over the fort, Sam heard rumors that some of the colonists planned to take the *Discovery* at night, load her with the colony's supplies, and return to England.

When Sam asked his master about the rumors, Smith frowned. "No one will take the ship if I can prevent it! We can't spare any of our supplies, especially with winter approaching," he said. "Taking our supplies or one of our ships is stealing, plain and simple. By English law, we punish thieves severely."

For the most part, John Smith ignored the campfire complaints. While others grumbled, he organized work parties. Smith was convinced that some of the sickness was caused by sleeping on the damp ground, and he knew the colonists would need better housing when the weather turned cold. He urged the men to build houses so they could discard the moldy, threadbare tents. To keep a supply of food coming from the Indians, Smith encouraged James Read, the blacksmith, to make small tools out of iron so the colonists had something to trade.

But the rumors multiplied. Since Smith was now a member of the council, many of the men complained to him about the president. "Look at Master Wingfield, would ye? How come he's still got his weight and strength? All the rest of us have been dropping like flies!"

Sam was often at Smith's side, and he overheard many of these conversations. Sam knew that some of the colonists suspected that President Wingfield had put aside food for himself and his favorites, while other men were starving. He even heard rumors that Wingfield was plotting to steal the ship and set up another colony in a different location!

Although John Smith disliked sitting idly in conversation, Sam noticed that he listened patiently to every complaint about Master Wingfield—no matter how petty. *Master Smith never brushes aside the men when they complain about the president. He's not sorry that Master Wingfield has lost everybody's respect!*

To put an end to the rumors, the council met to hear evidence against Wingfield. The councilmen decided to remove Master Wingfield from the presidency and from the council. Master Wingfield was placed in custody on the *Discovery* until all the accusations against him could be investigated. At the same time, George Kendall was released from confinement, since no further evidence had been found to support the accusations against him.

Now, the colony needed a new president. John Ratcliffe was the last remaining ship's captain, so he was the natural choice.

The councilmen also acknowledged Smith's talents. Since he was such an energetic and able organizer, they appointed him cape merchant, the officer in charge of supplies and equipment.

As cape merchant, Smith's first concern was finding and storing enough food to last the winter. He directed a group of workmen to strengthen the colony's storehouse. Smith told Sam and Nate to work alongside the men, since carpentry was a useful skill for the boys to learn.

The boys carried buckets of mud up from the river, and the men packed the mud around a frame of woven saplings to make the storehouse walls. When the walls were thick and sturdy, Smith instructed the men to build plenty of shelving to keep a winter's supply of food from rotting on the ground. He checked carefully to be sure that the thatch on the roof was dense and even, so rain could not seep in and dampen the sacks of corn and beans.

The storehouse completed, Smith divided the workers into teams to build sleeping quarters. Sam watched with longing every night when other colonists ducked inside their new houses to bed down. Smith insisted that he and the boys would remain in a tent every night until all the others had permanent sleeping quarters. That way, nobody could accuse him of making himself comfortable at the expense of others.

Now that the settlers were able to hunt and fish, the Indians gradually stopped bringing gifts of vegetables and game. So the Englishmen bartered iron tools to obtain a supply of dried corn and beans from the Indians. But after a while the neighboring Indians had as many iron tools as they could use, and they refused to trade any more, since they would need their food to get through the winter.

Each day, Smith checked the storehouse and estimated how much food remained. Soon, the fort's food supplies had dwindled to only enough for a few weeks, and Smith volunteered to lead a trading party. He planned to take the shallop to an Indian village farther down the river, thinking that the natives who lived some distance from the fort would still be interested in trading corn for iron tools.

Smith chose seven of his best workers for the journey. He told Sam to load the shallop with his iron helmet, breastplate, gun, and provisions for several days. "And put in a helmet and breastplate for yourself, too."

"And what about Nate?" Sam asked. "Can we take him on the trip, too? Please, Master Smith. He's been so miserable since Master Calthrop died."

Smith raised his eyebrows, and Sam wished he'd held his tongue. He was only a boy. It wasn't his place to tell his master what he should or shouldn't do.

To Sam's relief, Smith nodded. "Yes, Sam, Nate can come along," he said. "You don't need to worry. Now that he's on his own, I intend to watch out for him. Nate's a fine lad, and I appreciate how he looked after you—and me, for that matter—when the sickness was upon us. As I see where his talents lie, I'll assign him a trade to study, so he'll be assured of a livelihood. We need all kinds of craftsmen here in Virginia. Meanwhile, he can come along with us. I feel sure he'll make himself useful."

The trading party set out, heading down the James River toward Chesapeake Bay. Sam remembered that the Kecoughtan Indians lived at the mouth of the river, and that they had welcomed the colonists when they first landed in Virginia.

When the shallop reached Kecoughtan, Smith left two men to guard the boat and took the others to visit the village. The chief was polite and offered them some corn cakes. He was willing to trade a few handfuls of dried beans for a hatchet, but he seemed uninterested in any further bartering.

Some of the village children ran by and tossed scraps of food at Sam and Nate. Stamping his foot, Nate sent the children scampering away. "Do we look so ragged that they take us for charity cases?" he snarled. "It's a wonder that Master Smith stays here—we're being treated more like beggars than traders."

Sam shrugged. "Perhaps this is a poor village," he said, "and they don't have enough food to trade."

Nate squinted at Sam as if his friend had lost his senses. "Open your eyes, Sam. You saw that garden by the river!" he exclaimed. "It was full of squash, pumpkins, and beans. These villagers don't look like they're starving."

Nate is right, Sam thought. He was confused. *My master is acting like this is a social visit. He doesn't seem to care if the chief wants to trade.*

As Smith led their group back to the river, he pulled aside one gentleman. "Hide in these bushes," he told the man. "Keep a close watch. Find out how much food the villagers have stored and where it's kept. Estimate how many warriors live here. We've come to get food for our settlement, and I will not return empty-handed. If these Indians aren't willing to make a fair trade, then we'll take what we need!"

After dark, the gentleman returned to the shallop. He reported that the village consisted of about eighteen houses spread across three acres of fertile plain, and the Indians had plenty of food. Early the next morning, Smith ordered the sailors to haul up the anchor and take the shallop out to the middle of the river. There, he told his men to put on their helmets and breastplates and make ready to fire their guns. He ordered the sailors to row with all their strength, until they ran the boat onto the shore in front of the village. Immediately, Smith ordered his men to open fire, and the Indians fled screaming for cover.

Sam and Nate marched behind Smith and the others into the empty village. The boys' eyes were round with amazement.

"Has your master gone mad?" Nate whispered. "These savages aren't going to let us march in and seize their food. They're sure to attack us! There aren't even ten of us, and they've got a village full of warriors. They'll kill every one of us!"

Before Sam had a chance to answer, seventy Indians rushed out of the woods, chanting. Their faces and chests were streaked with black, red, and white paint, and they carried clubs as well as bows and arrows. When all the Indians were in the open, they stood and faced the little row of Englishmen. So many armed warriors! Their scowling faces and bright paint made them look ferocious. Sam feared his knees would collapse and he would fall to the ground.

Suddenly, one of the Indians held up a statue shaped like a man. It was made of stuffed skins and decorated with copper chains. With the statue held at arm's length in front of his face, he began a different chant. All at once, the Indians charged!

Smith stood his ground and yelled, "Fire!"

The blast from their guns instantly stopped the charge. Several warriors fell to the ground, howling. In the confusion, the Indian in front dropped the statue. As the Englishmen reloaded, the Indians scurried into the woods, moaning and screaming.

A little while later, one of the Indians came out of the woods, his face and chest wiped clean of paint. He bowed respectfully to Smith and pointed to the statue, which he called *okee*. Smith gestured for the Indian to fill the boat with food. He said he'd give up the statue and also give beads, hatchets, and copper in return for food.

Shortly afterward, six Indians appeared, each holding baskets of food. They loaded the shallop with dried corn, venison, wild turkeys, and corn cakes. When they were finished, Smith gave the Indians the trade goods he had promised, and he returned the statue. Then he boarded the shallop to return to the fort.

As they headed up the river, Nate sat in the stern and stared at the water. When Sam approached him, Nate snapped, "Your master risked our lives in that village. What if the savages hadn't run away after we fired our guns?"

Sam defended Smith, and the two boys quarreled.

"What's wrong, lads?" Smith called.

Both boys fell silent. They didn't speak to each other again until they reached the fort.

Although Sam didn't really understand why his master had decided to attack the village, he waited until that night when he brought Smith his supper to ask. "I counted more than seventy warriors in that village, Master Smith," Sam said. "But we had less than ten grown men, counting the two who were guarding our shallop. What if the Kecoughtans had continued to fight?"

"We have guns, Sam, and the Indians don't," Smith said. "And we had the benefit of surprise. I was confident of the outcome."

Sam paused, trying to think of a way to express what else was on his mind. *Isn't it a crime to attack a village? Isn't it stealing to take food by force? Those goods that we gave in exchange for all that food were of little value.* What Sam really wanted to ask was: Now that we've treated the Indians so badly, mightn't they resume their attacks on our fort?

Smith seemed to understand what was bothering Sam. "Lad, I've traveled in many lands," he said, "and I've learned that people won't respect you unless you show them your strength. When the Kecoughtan chief saw us coming peaceably—to offer goods in trade for food—he treated us like beggars and tossed a few crumbs at us. I knew we'd never get a fair trade as long as the Indians consider us weaklings. We had to show our might.

"Mark my words, Sam. The chief of Kecoughtan will respect us in the future. And news of our boldness will spread to the other Indian villages, as well." Smith met the boy's gaze. "Do you understand?"

Sam didn't reply. He lowered his eyes. He didn't dare offend Smith, but he did think his master had been reckless with the lives of his own men and cruel to the Indians.

Smith laughed. "You think I'm wrong, don't you?" Smith clapped his hand on Sam's shoulder. "Well, Sam, wait and see how the Indians treat us next time we send out a trading party."

During the autumn, English trading parties traveled up and down the river. Usually, John Smith led them, and Sam went along. Sam watched the Indian chiefs greet Smith with great courtesy. In fact, Smith was able to make much better deals than the other English traders. Among the Indians, Smith was treated as if he was the head of James Fort.

In the fort, Smith's reputation grew among the laborers. Every time his trading parties returned with bushels of corn, the men cheered. The shelves in the storehouse filled up with food. Sam felt sure their settlement could now survive the winter, even if a supply ship from England did not reach Virginia before cold weather set in. The little plot of wheat that Smith had insisted the settlers plant yielded a small but welcome crop. The new buildings made the fort seem a sturdier place, a place with some permanence.

But Sam noticed an undercurrent of unrest in the fort. Not all of the settlers were satisfied. Conversations halted abruptly when Sam walked by. Some of the gentlemen were whispering about John Smith, Sam was sure of it. He asked Nate what the men were saying.

"That your master is bossy and arrogant!" Nate replied. "That he enjoys giving orders to men of higher status."

"You don't feel that way about Master Smith, do you?"

Nate paused. "No," he said at last. "I respect Master Smith, Sam. I really do. But sometimes I've thought that he's a hard man to like."

Sam pretended that he didn't notice the whispers about his master. But they made him nervous. These vague resentments had turned deadly before. How could he forget the gallows in the West Indies?

The lush green of summer began to thin, and at night the air became cool and pleasant. At last, the daytime weather turned crisp. Sam noticed that when he walked through the woods, the fallen leaves crunched beneath his feet. He had a clear view of Virginia's blue sky, even when he was in dense forest. Soon the mornings were cold enough for Sam to see his breath when he left the sleeping quarters.

The autumn weather didn't cool the men's tempers, though. George Kendall was back to his old ways, stirring up discontent among the colonists. Sam often saw him talking with little clusters of gentlemen. Whenever Sam or John Smith came near, the men shifted their gaze and lowered their voices. Kendall wasn't permitted to carry a gun because his name had never been completely cleared. But his words were just as persuasive as before.

Now that his master was out and about, Richard Mutton returned to his old habits, too. He snickered whenever he saw Sam at work. Sam wished he'd spoken his mind when Master Kendall was under arrest. *If I'd given him a taste of his own medicine,* Sam thought, *maybe he wouldn't act so snotty now.*

Oddly enough, George Kendall was becoming very friendly with the colony's new president, John Ratcliffe. He even moved into the president's house. Ratcliffe went so far as to put Kendall in charge of the next trading expedition.

"How can Master Kendall lead a trading expedition?" Sam asked Smith. "I thought he wasn't allowed to carry a weapon."

Smith snorted, his nostrils flaring, but he didn't answer. Sam noticed that his master's jaw tightened whenever Kendall's name was mentioned in a conversation. Since Kendall had become President Ratcliffe's constant companion, Smith kept his distance from both men.

One day, an argument broke out between President Ratcliffe and one of the laborers, James Read the blacksmith. The argument grew heated, and Read insulted the president.

"Look here, man!" Ratcliffe shouted. "As president of this colony, I will not put up with insolence from a worker." Ratcliffe slapped Read's face. He called a guard and said, "I want you to restrain this man."

When the guard reached for Read, the blacksmith became furious. He shoved aside the guard, punched Ratcliffe in the stomach, and knocked him to the ground. The president staggered to his feet, and Read lunged for Ratcliffe's neck. It took several men to pull the blacksmith away.

"Come near me again, and I'll shove this anvil down your throat!" Read screamed. "I'll kill you—president or not!"

Ratcliffe gasped, "You're threatening me? You scoundrel! I'll have your tongue silenced once and for all!"

Read was quickly tried, found guilty of insubordination, and condemned to death. To save his life, he volunteered to reveal a mutiny.

According to the blacksmith, George Kendall was at the heart of the plot. Kendall had stolen supplies from the storehouse and loaded them aboard the *Discovery*. Under the guise of outfitting the ship for a trading party, Kendall was secretly planning to head for England!

Kendall was already aboard ship when the councilmen heard the blacksmith's story. Rushing to the guard platform, they ordered Kendall to come ashore. He resisted until the fort's cannon was pointed at the ship. After he surrendered, the councilmen searched the ship. Sure enough, they discovered letters, stolen goods, and other evidence. Kendall was bound, tried, and convicted. Found guilty of mutiny, he was shot to death.

Sam was stunned. "They've executed an Englishman! A gentleman!" he said to Nate. "Half of our men have already died from sickness or Indian attacks. With so few settlers left, I don't think the council ought to put a man to death as a punishment. Do you? Master Kendall suffered through the seasoning, just like the rest of us."

Nate shrugged. "George Kendall deserved to die. He was a spy and a traitor. He got caught stealing that ship and our supplies, didn't he? He was planning to leave the rest of us here to starve. Why waste your pity on such a man?" Nate stared vacantly into the trees. "So many others have died. Innocent men, who suffered and died in pain—those are the men I pity."

When Sam questioned John Smith about the matter, his master's tone was matter-of-fact. "Kendall wasn't the first criminal who disguised himself in the clothes of an English gentleman, Sam. And he won't be the last. That matter is done, and good riddance, I say. We've got the future to look to. Our food stocks have been rescued from Kendall's thieving hands, but we haven't got enough in the storehouse to last the winter. We need to send out another trading party, and soon. It's already December. I don't know how long the weather will accommodate travel."

Sam stared at John Smith. *He's happy! My master is happy that George Kendall was convicted and put to death,* Sam realized. Then he examined his own feelings. *It is a relief to know that Kendall isn't walking around anymore, whispering behind Master Smith's back, stirring up trouble.* Sam shuddered. *What's happening to me? What's happening to all of us?*

Trading Terror

John Smith took charge of the trading party. He set out on December 10 with nine men and the boys, Sam and Nate. His goal was to trade with the Indians and to explore the Chickahominy River in hopes of discovering gold and precious minerals.

The Chickahominy flowed into the James a few miles north and west of the fort. Its banks were lined with red and yellow clay and bounded by fields of rich, black soil. Sam had never seen as many fish as he found in these waters, and the waterfowl were just as plentiful as the fish. The shores were dotted by Indian villages whose inhabitants seemed to thrive on the richness of their land.

The party traveled forty miles up the Chickahominy, passing a large village that the Indians called Apokant. Ten miles further, the river narrowed into a swiftly flowing stream. Afraid their boat would run aground, Smith ordered the men to turn around and anchor near the village. He went ashore and hired a canoe and two Indian guides. He took two men with him, a gentleman named John Robinson and Thomas Emry, a carpenter. All three took their guns so they could hunt for wildfowl. Smith told the others to stay on the boat until he returned.

Sam and Nate waited aboard the boat with the seven remaining men. They fished and cooked over a little fire in an iron pot on deck. That night, they slept aboard the boat. All the next day, the boys watched the activity along the shore beside the village. By nightfall, both boys and men were as restless as caged animals.

"I say let's have a look at the land around the village," said a laborer named George Cassen. "We could be here for days waiting for the captain. We've got to do something while we wait."

"Captain Smith told us to wait on the boat," another man said. "Those were his orders."

"That he did," Cassen retorted. "But Captain Smith hates idleness more than he hates poison. What harm could come from doing a bit of hunting?"

In the end, Cassen won, mainly because the men were tired of being cooped up in the boat. They pulled up anchor and rowed the boat to shore fifty yards upriver from the village. Cassen cut seven small reeds and trimmed them to the same length, then shortened one of them. He told Sam to hold the reeds so the shortened end was concealed in his hand.

Each man drew a reed, and as luck would have it, Cassen drew the short one. He had to stay by the boat as guard, while the others divided into two groups to explore the woods near the river. The men took their guns, but they left their armor on board because the day was unseasonably warm and because the villagers seemed peaceful enough. Before the groups separated, they agreed to use a birdcall as a signal, in case somebody needed help or Smith's canoe was spotted.

Two of the men told Sam and Nate to come with them. Sam was keenly aware of the noises they made as they tramped over the brittle twigs and dry leaves. He worried about leaving the boat against Master Smith's orders and about hunting so close to the Indian village. But the men had made up their minds to go on shore, and they hadn't given the boys any choice about going along.

After walking for about thirty minutes, Sam's group stepped into a clearing with a pond in the middle. The pond was teeming with geese.

The hunters spread out. Sam moved to the right and crept through the trees to the far side of the pond. Taking care not to alarm the geese, he pushed through some bushes and waited. He thought he heard a far-off birdcall—the signal the men had agreed to use if somebody needed help. Sam crouched down and listened carefully, but he didn't hear another birdcall. *Has one of the men met some Indians?* he wondered.

Suddenly a shot rang out. A clatter of honking and splashing came from the pond. Sam heard Nate's voice: "Got it!"

Sam rushed into the clearing and spotted Nate by the side of the pond. He was dragging a limp goose out of the water with a branch. Running to Nate's side, Sam helped his friend haul the big bird out of the water. The men joined them.

"The other birds have flown," one of them said. "Heading west." He turned to Nate. "Next time you go hunting, lad, wait until everybody's ready before you shoot. The noise frightens the rest of the flock, and they all fly off."

The group walked in a westerly direction for a few hours, but never came upon any signs of geese. When the sunlight slanted low through the trees, they turned back. They reached the shore of the Chickahominy as dusk was falling. The other group of hunters was already on board.

"Where's Cassen?" they asked, as soon as Sam's group climbed aboard.

"What do you mean? I thought he was guarding the ship."

"He wasn't here when we got back. We thought maybe he was with you."

"How long have you been back here?"

"Less than an hour."

Sam could tell that the men were worried, but nobody voiced what was on their minds.

"I thought I heard a birdcall when we were at that pond," Sam said. "Did any of you signal?"

The men looked at each other. One man said, "It didn't come from our group. Maybe it was Cassen."

"Why didn't you mention it before, lad?" asked a man from Sam's group.

"I wasn't sure if it really was a signal. Then Nate shot the goose, and I never thought about it again—until now."

The men frowned. They glanced at the woods and squinted at the path leading toward the village.

"I knew we should've stayed on the river. Like the cap'n ordered," one man grumbled, shaking his head.

"What's done is done," said another. "I say we pull up anchor and get out of here. Before them savages come after us."

Sam was astonished. "We can't just leave," he gasped. "What will happen to Cassen? And Master Smith? He and Master Robinson and Emry may be back any time now. We told them we'd meet them here."

One of the men scowled at Sam. "We can't afford to put this boat in danger, boy. It looks to me like the savages ambushed George Cassen. I'm thinking that John Smith and the others are already taken prisoner. They could be dead by now, for all we know. I say we head back to the fort and thank our lucky stars if we make it alive."

"I won't abandon Master Smith!" Sam said in a voice so loud that he surprised himself. He looked at Nate for support.

Nate shrugged. "Cassen could be in Apokant," he said reasonably. "The Indians could have invited him to eat with them. Shouldn't we wait and find out what's going on before we run away?"

The men's voices were tense. "Cassen wouldn't just leave the boat—against orders."

"We all left the boat, against orders," Sam blurted out.

"Look, boy, it's easy to talk brave. Are you willin' to go into the village and see if Cassen is there?" demanded one of the men.

Sam stared at them. *They're cowards,* he thought. *I wish I hadn't gone along with them when they disobeyed my master's orders.* "Yes!" Sam said, his voice trembling. "I'll go."

Nate jumped to his feet and stepped to Sam's side.

"No, Nate. I'm going alone," Sam said. "Two will make more noise than one."

Sam turned to the men. "I'll sneak into the village. If I find Cassen and he's safe, I'll give a shout so you'll know there's no need to worry. But if Cassen is in trouble, I'll come back as soon as I can. You take the boat out to the middle of the river and drop anchor to wait for me. I'll throw rocks into the water to let you know where I am, so you can pick me up."

"And since when does a servant boy give orders to grown men?" one man snarled.

Another man shrugged, "The lad's plan sounds fine to me. If he's willin' to sneak into the savages' village to look for Cassen, I say let him. Tell you one thing—*I'm* not about to volunteer for the job!"

One of the men glared at Sam. "If we don't hear from you by daybreak, we're taking the boat back to the fort."

Sam nodded and locked eyes with Nate. He knew that Nate wouldn't let the men break their word and leave without waiting for him. But if something happened and Sam couldn't return by morning....

Knowing it was best to travel as lightly as possible, Sam put down the heavy gun that he'd been carrying. He took off his shoes and left them on the ship. Before he scrambled onto shore, Nate handed him a knife.

Sam picked his way through trees and underbrush toward the village. It would have been easier to make his way along the shore, but he didn't want the Indians to see him coming. As soon as he left the sounds of the river and entered the woods, he could hear voices. They were continuous, sometimes rising into odd yips, sometimes falling into a low chant. When he reached the edge of the village, the houses looked deserted. Sam saw smoke rising from a clearing between the dwellings. The voices were coming from that direction. Darting from tree to tree, he finally got close enough to see.

George Cassen was standing naked in front of a large fire, his back against two stakes in the ground. His hands and feet were bound to the stakes with thick ropes, and his toes were practically touching the flames. Cassen's body was shining in the firelight. Sweat plastered down his hair, and his head sagged on his chest. Blood ran in glistening streaks down his arms and legs.

Sam held his breath. The village women were circling the fire, holding large shells. As they danced in and out, they chanted. Every few minutes, one of the women raised her voice and make that odd yipping sound while she lunged and jabbed Cassen with the sharp edge of her shell. The Englishman screamed when the shells cut his skin. The men of the village sat on mats watching the spectacle. Their faces and chests were painted, and they chanted along with the women. Sam's hand closed tightly over the handle of his knife, and he looked around wildly for something he could do to make the torture stop.

Suddenly, one of the women let out an ear-piercing shriek and made a stab at Cassen's head. She swooped and tore at his earlobe, then waved her fist in front of Cassen's eyes before heaving the bloody lump into the fire. Cassen roared, then cried out in a voice choked with sobs, "Stop, I beg of you!"

Sam backed up and stumbled into the trees, praying the Indians didn't hear him. Trembling all over, he leaned against a trunk. His head began to swim, and he held onto the rough bark. Then he leaned over and vomited. The stench of his vomit mingled with the image of Cassen's torture, and Sam heaved again and again until his stomach was empty.

I have to get help, Sam thought. *I'm just one boy armed with a knife. I can't rescue poor Cassen from a whole village by myself.*

Trying to move quickly without alerting the Indians, Sam threaded his way through the trees in what he hoped was the direction of the river. After what seemed like hours, he reached the shore. He saw the boat shining on the water in the moonlight, but it lay at anchor some thirty feet from shore and at least two hundred feet upriver from where he stood. To get closer to it, Sam would have to walk across the exposed waterfront in front of the village. Or he would have to skirt all the way around the other side of the village through the trees. He thought it was too dangerous to try either way.

Instead, Sam gathered a handful of small stones and began flinging them into the water. They pinged and splashed. In the still of the night, the sounds seemed louder than trumpets. He glanced over his shoulders, expecting to see the villagers dash out of the trees to grab him. He didn't see any movement around him, but he couldn't spot any movement on the boat, either. *Can the guard on board hear the splashing at this distance?*

Sam searched for something larger to throw. He found a dead branch and heaved it as far as he could into the water, hoping the bigger splash would catch the attention of the night guard. But still there was no activity on deck. Finally, Sam cupped his hands around his mouth and let out the birdcall that the group used as a distress signal.

Sam strained to see. *Are the men on deck now? Are they pulling up the anchor?* Sam waited, breathlessly, alert to any sounds behind him. His mind raced, trying to decide on the best course of action. *Should I run into the trees and hide until the boat approaches? What if Indians are in the trees, waiting to grab me? Maybe I should jump into the river and try to swim for the boat. Can I make it that far in the cold water?*

Suddenly, Sam heard a snap behind him. In an instant, he plunged into the river.

The icy water pierced Sam's skin. Concentrating on the sight of the boat, he kicked his legs and forced his arms to reach as far as they could with every stroke. He shut his eyes, held his breath, and stuck his face in the river, praying for the strength to keep stroking. When he brought his face up for air, he couldn't believe how far away the boat seemed. He lost feeling in his hands and feet, but his chest screamed from the stabbing cold. At last, he caught sight of a person kneeling on the side of the boat, looking at the water. Sam gasped for air and called out. Then he focused on swimming—he commanded his arms to keep stroking, his legs to keep kicking. He could feel his body sinking lower with every stroke.

Sam heard a splash. Somebody had jumped into the water! Sam felt strong arms grasping him. He was being pulled through the water. His fingers touched the wood of the boat, and he struggled to grab hold. Somebody was pushing him. Up, up. Two men grabbed his collar and hauled him aboard. Then they reached down and helped the other swimmer scramble aboard. Nate collapsed on deck beside Sam in a puddle of cold water.

"They've got Cassen. They're torturing him," Sam sputtered, water streaming down his back, his teeth chattering wildly.

"That's it, then! We're heading for the fort," one of the men cried.

"But we can't leave him here," Sam gasped. "They're killing him. The women are stabbing him with shells. I saw them. They cut off his ear...."

Ignoring Sam, the men hauled up the anchor and unfurled the sail. The boat began to pick up speed.

"But we've got guns," Sam protested. "We can fire at them. We can surprise them."

He struggled to his feet and made a grab for the ropes that held the sail. One of the men shoved him out of the way. Sam's head smacked against something hard on the deck, and pain washed over him. Nate leaped across the deck and kneeled over him.

The man secured the sail, then tossed a blanket to Nate and covered Sam with another. "We have six men and a pair of boys," he said. "We haven't a chance against a village full of savages. If we try to get Cassen, they'll kill us all. We've got to get back to the fort."

"What about my master?" Sam wailed.

"We haven't seen Master Smith for three days, Sam," Nate said, his voice low and grim. "He's probably dead by now. And Master Robinson and Emry with him."

New Year, New Promise

The savages are making sport of us!" President Ratcliffe declared when the trading party returned with four men missing. "We never should have trusted them."

The other council members nodded. "We should have known the savages meant no kindness when they brought food to our settlement. It was just another trick. They intend to keep us alive only to toy with us."

"Aye. Before they make an end to us, they'll tease us the way cats tease their prey."

The councilmen listened closely to the trading party's description of their disastrous trip. When Sam told them about the torture of Cassen, all of their fears were rekindled.

One of the councilmen buried his face in his hands. "Oh, dear God! They mean to kill us off, one by one—to torture us, like they did poor Cassen."

With a solemn face, President Ratcliffe shifted the discussion to other matters. Cold weather was coming on, their food was running low, and there'd been no word from Captain Newport. "If the situation does not improve, I doubt that our colony can survive the winter," he said. "And now that we have word the savages have resumed their hostilities—"

Sam interrupted to remind them that his master and Robinson and Emry were missing, but Ratcliffe ignored him. "If you send a search party," Sam persisted, "I can show you the place where we last saw—"

"Silence!" Ratcliffe shouted. "You are disrupting a meeting of this council."

The meeting continued. Expecting trouble, Ratcliffe announced that he would post an additional guard. He appointed Gabriel Archer to serve on the council in Smith's place.

As the meeting broke up, Reverend Hunt laid a hand on Sam's shoulder. "I know how worried you are about Master Smith, lad."

"Everybody seems to think my master is dead," Sam said. "But what if he's still alive? He's in terrible danger! He'll be searching the Chickahominy River for the trading party, and he has no way of knowing what the Apokant villagers did to George Cassen."

Hunt nodded. "I know, Sam. But our colony can't afford to risk one of the boats. And it's too dangerous to send out a search party on foot. We wouldn't know where to look."

"I could go with them. I could show them where the boat was anchored."

"Sam, even if you could locate the village by foot, do you really think you could find your master in all that wilderness?" Hunt looked in Sam's eyes.

For a few seconds, Sam held the clergyman's gaze. But he knew he couldn't find Apokant by himself, and certainly not on foot. Slowly, Sam lowered his eyes.

"I'm sorry, Sam. But our best course is to trust in the Lord to guide those poor men back to our fort safely. If they're still alive."

The weather turned bitterly cold. Because the fort's supplies were so low, food was severely rationed. The colonists got one hot meal a day of watery gruel made from dried beans and corn. In addition to the soup, they each got a small hunk of bread. Sam wolfed down his portion, but he felt hungry and cold all the time.

If Master Smith is alive, he's colder and hungrier than I am, Sam thought. *But if the Indians have him....* Sam's mind kept picturing Cassen being tortured by the Apokant women.

Sam hated to think about John Smith suffering, but it was worse to think about him being dead. *My family is thousands of miles away,* he thought. *Without Smith, I might as well be an orphan.*

The men in the fort avoided Sam. *Cowards!* he thought. *They feel guilty because they're afraid to send out a search party.* Even though he resented the men, he understood how helpless they felt. By day, thoughts of John Smith's plight and Cassen's torture haunted Sam, and he woke with terrible nightmares nearly every night.

After hearing about what happened to the trading party, the councilmen were too frightened to try again. As the last weeks of 1607 inched by, the shelves in the storehouse grew emptier every day. Unless a supply ship reached Virginia, the settlers were all doomed to die a slow death from starvation. The men moped around the fort. *They're waiting to die,* Sam thought, *and I've got no choice but to wait, too.*

Sam found that talking to Nate was no help. Whenever Sam mentioned his worries about Smith being dead or their colony starving, Nate shrugged. Looking straight ahead, Nate repeated the words, "James Fort is a place of death."

One afternoon, Sam was assigned guard duty at the north corner. He replaced the guard, slipping the man's slow match over his breastplate and fastening the shot pouch around his own waist. In accordance with orders, Sam took a piece of shot and popped it into his mouth, where he held it ready in case he needed to reload quickly. Then he knelt to pick up his helmet and gun. When he straightened up, the guard on duty with him was waving to Richard Mutton, who had just stepped out of a nearby building.

"Come here, lad," the guard called to Richard. "Take my place on the platform. I'll be back as soon as I've answered nature's call." The guard handed his gun and ammunition to Richard and jumped off the platform.

Sam and Richard looked warily at one another, then Sam moved as far away from Richard as he could get on the small platform. Sam concentrated on scanning the landscape and the river for unusual movements. Richard said something, but Sam couldn't make out the words. Richard spoke again, in a louder voice. His tone was so gentle, so unlike anything Sam had ever heard from him, that Sam whirled around in surprise.

"I guess it's harder on you than it is on me—or on Peacock," Richard said. "At least we know for sure that our masters are dead and gone. That's probably easier than not knowing."

Sam didn't speak. He stared at Richard, too amazed to nod.

Richard eyed Sam sheepishly. When his words were greeted with silence, Richard turned away and fiddled with his slow match.

A few minutes later, Richard said, "I don't blame you for hating me, Samuel Collier. But there aren't very many of us left here. There may come a day when we'll need to speak to each other. Anyway, what's the use of holding a grudge as we go to the grave?"

"I'm not going to the grave!" Sam declared, his voice colder than he had intended.

"Well, I'm not wishing death on you," Richard said. "You needn't be so cross."

"I haven't wished death on you, either," Sam said, then caught himself. *Maybe I have wished him dead,* Sam thought. *He is a spiteful bully.*

"You haven't?" Mutton asked, his eyebrows flying upward in surprise.

Richard's expression struck Sam as comical. He gave a sudden laugh and the lead shot pitched out of his mouth. It clattered onto the platform, and Sam bent over to grab it. But the shot rolled toward Richard, who retrieved it and handed it back to him.

"Thank you," Sam said stiffly. He turned away and concentrated on the river.

In a few minutes, the guard returned to the platform, thanked Richard, and resumed his duty. Sam said nothing as Richard hopped off the platform and walked away.

A few days later, Sam and Nate were sent to gather firewood. Since the settlers had already cut and cleared most of the wood around the fort, the boys had to walk a fair distance. They walked slowly, alert for any signs of Indians. They hadn't brought guns because they needed their hands free for their task.

"Wait up!" a voice called.

The boys turned to see Richard running to catch up to them.

"Where do you think you're going?" Nate demanded. "Nobody invited you."

"Master Ratcliffe ordered me to collect firewood," Richard said. "He told me to catch up with you two, because nobody is supposed to leave the fort alone."

Nate scowled. "We can gather enough firewood without your help," he said. "I know how you love to watch other people work, Richard—so you can sneer at them. But I can't abide you or your sneering. Why don't you go back to the fort and find somebody else to annoy?"

Richard's face turned purple, and Sam braced himself for a scuffle. Instead, the bully's shoulders sagged, and he wheeled around.

The boys had taken only a few more steps when Richard

called after them: "I had nothing to do with the death of your master, Nathaniel Peacock!"

Nate froze.

"What are you talking about?" Sam yelled. "Master Calthrop died of the sickness."

"I've heard the talk around the fort," Richard said. "There are those who claim that certain gentlemen kept the best food for themselves and their friends. That other men—like Nate's master—might have been spared from death if they'd gotten some of the food that had been selfishly set aside. But I swear I never got a bigger portion than the next fellow!" Richard continued. "If Master Kendall ever took more than his fair share, he didn't give any extra to me. I wasn't treated any better than anybody else."

Richard lowered his eyes and Sam studied him. Richard was much thinner than he'd been when they'd arrived in Virginia. His shoulders sagged, pulling his chest inward. He didn't look so sure of himself as he used to. "Master Kendall didn't tell me his secrets, you know," Richard continued. "I never even knew that he was plotting to steal a ship and head for England."

Sam took a step toward Richard. "Do you think your master would have left you here by yourself?"

"I don't know," Richard said, and his voice choked. "Maybe he would have taken me with him. A few days before he was caught, he asked me if I'd like to go back to England."

"What did you answer?" Sam asked. "Did you say you wanted to go back?"

"I said no. That I thought I'd do fine here, in spite of the sickness. I didn't want my master to think I was a weakling." Richard looked away. "But I was just talking big. If I had the chance to go back now, I'd go quicker than you can say Virginia. I hate this place."

"I do, too," Nate whispered. "I wish I'd never set eyes on James Fort. I'd give anything to go back to England."

Sam stared at Nate. This was the first time he'd heard his best friend say he wanted to give up and go back to England.

"What about you, Sam Collier?" Richard asked. "Do you wish you could go back to England?"

Sam was speechless. He'd never considered the possibility of going back. He remembered how he used to boast that he was the luckiest boy in England because Master Smith had chosen to take him to Virginia. That he'd never return to the old country—that England was dirty and worn out. Sam thought about his father's farm in Lincolnshire, the farm that his brother Thomas would inherit. It seemed so small, now that he had seen the open spaces of this new world.

What would I do if I went back to England? I won't inherit the farm, so how would I scrape together a living? Sam thought. *But I haven't seen any easy riches here in Virginia, either. All I've seen is death and suffering. Suffering more horrible than anything I'd ever imagined!*

Sam looked at Richard and answered, "I don't know if I'd go back to England." And that was the truth.

There was no feast that Christmas in James Fort. The colonists huddled around fires in their wooden huts, trying to keep warm. On the first day of January 1608, they rang in the new year on the same solemn note as they bid farewell to the old. Reverend Hunt led a prayer service. Then the good minister made the rounds of the sick.

Early the next morning, Sam and Nate were crossing the frosty ground outside the fort in search of dead branches for firewood. As they walked, they blew on their fingers to keep them from freezing. They'd been out nearly an hour when they heard footsteps. Instantly alert to danger, they slipped behind some trees and waited.

"Sam! Samuel Collier!" shouted a voice. "Sam! It's me—Richard. I have news of your master!"

Sam caught Nate's eye. Bracing himself for bad news, he called, "Over here!"

Richard ran toward them, panting and red-faced. "John Smith's back." He paused to catch his breath. "He...he's safe!"

Sam dropped his wood and took off running toward the fort.

Nate and Richard followed. "What about Master Robinson and Thomas Emry?" Nate shouted.

"They didn't come back."

When the boys reached the fort, Sam saw a crowd of men outside President Ratcliffe's lodging. He pushed his way inside. John Smith was sitting on a bench surrounded by the council. The men stopped talking as Sam rushed to his master's side.

Smith looked remarkably healthy. His clothing was tattered, but his weight and color gave no indication that he'd been suffering. In fact, Sam thought his master looked heartier than the men who had spent the last month in James Fort.

As soon as Smith saw Sam, he stopped talking and clasped the boy's shoulders. He said, "Well, Samuel Collier, you're a sight for sore eyes. Many a night these past weeks, I wondered if I would ever gaze upon you again while we dwelled on this earth."

President Ratcliffe cleared his throat, and Sam realized he'd barged into the middle of a council meeting. An entire room full of gentlemen was staring at him! All at once, he was aware that teardrops were sliding down his cheeks. He felt his neck grow warm, and he knew his cheeks had turned red. Ashamed, he lowered his eyes.

Smith motioned for Sam to sit on the floor by his knee.

"I saw only one of the bodies," Smith said, resuming his tale. "When my captors led me back to the site of our campfire, John Robinson was lying on the ground near the canoe. He had twenty or thirty arrows in him. As for Emry—I never saw his body, but the Indians had set fires all over the woods. I suppose his corpse was consumed in the blaze."

"And would you do us the courtesy," President Ratcliffe said sharply, "to explain how you, Master Smith—the commander in charge of the trading party—came to be separated from your men?"

"As I told you," Smith said, "a few days after we hired the Indians and their canoe, we made our evening camp. Our supper was boiling over the fire when I decided to survey the nature of the soil. I took one of our Indian guides with me. I left the other Indian guide with Robinson and Emry. Before leaving, I made sure my men had their guns on their laps and their matches lit. I ordered them to fire if they caught sight of any Indians near the camp.

"I had been gone about a quarter of an hour when I heard a loud cry and shouting, but no gunfire. I guessed my men had been surprised by a band of Indians. Supposing our guides had betrayed us, I seized the fellow with me and tied his arm to mine so he could not run off. In truth, the fellow seemed as surprised as I was by the ambush. He urged me to run away. But before I could take flight, an arrow struck my right thigh. Fortunately, it glanced off without doing me harm. I whirled to see two Indians drawing their bows, and I fired my pistol at them. One fell down, and the other ran off.

"Three or four more Indians came at me. I fired again and pulled the Indian guide close against my back as a shield. At least twenty arrows were shot at me, but they fell short. I discharged my pistol three or four times before I was surrounded by about two hundred braves carrying drawn bows. They were led by their king, whose name is Opechancanough. Later, I found out that he is the brother of the mighty Powhatan."

Smith paused and looked around the room. Every man was absorbed in his story. Sam smiled, remembering the many nights he had listened to his master's stories of hair-raising adventures in Turkey and other faraway lands.

"And how was it that the savages were convinced to spare your life, Master Smith," Ratcliffe asked, "after they had murdered both of your companions?"

"My pistol was loaded, and I aimed it at my attackers. If the braves made a rush for me, I intended to kill as many of them as I could. My Indian guide was still fastened to my arm, and he began speaking. Said I was the captain of our party. The warriors seemed to understand him, so I told the fellow to let them know that all I wanted was to be allowed to leave their territory. That I would go peacefully. They commanded me to throw down my weapon, and this I refused. Stepping backward, I lost my balance and fell into a muddy hole. The braves closed in on me. They pulled away my Indian guide—I never found out what became of him. I decided my best hope was to try their mercy. So I threw aside my weapon and let them lead me to their king.

"I had a compass in my pouch, and I offered it to the king. He demanded to know how it was used, and I showed him. I drew pictures in the dirt to explain how the device helps a man locate his whereabouts. King Opechancanough has a lively mind, and he was intrigued. He tried out the compass, moving it around in a circle to watch the dial move. Then he seated himself upon a mat and bid me sit by him. The king asked me all sorts of questions. I told him about the roundness of this earth and the course of the sun, moon, stars, and planets. While he listened, the king ordered his attendants to bring me bread to eat. Then he made a speech welcoming me to his country, which is the land of the Pamunkeys. At my request, he conducted me to the camp where I'd left my men, and I saw the body of John Robinson. After that, I fully expected the Indians to execute me. But instead, they took me to their village, which is about six miles from where I was captured."

As soon as Smith said the word, "village," Sam remembered the village of Apokant. An image of George Cassen—his naked body tied to a stake and blood running down his arms and legs—flashed into his mind. Forgetting his manners, Sam burst out, "Did they torture you, Master Smith?"

"That's what I was expecting, Sam," Smith said. "But when we reached the village, all the women and children came out to greet us. The warriors formed lines and ran back and forth in some sort of display. Afterward, they formed a ring and danced. Then I was led to a fire, like a guest, and served a quarter of venison and about ten cakes of bread! What I could not eat was sent with me to King Opechancanough's lodging, where I was given shelter for the night.

"Each morning, three women served me, bringing me great platters of their bread and more venison than five men could devour. They returned my compass and everything they had taken from me, except my weapons. Although eight warriors guarded me at all times, the Pamunkeys did everything they could to make me comfortable.

"The king often came and spoke with me. He asked me questions about our ships and our fort and even about our God. I told him how strong our fort is. I described how Captain Newport was coming with more ships and more Englishmen. I told him that any Indians who attacked our fort would feel the terrible sting of our revenge."

"And you remained a prisoner—or rather a guest—of this King Opechancanough all these weeks? Since your capture?" Gabriel Archer asked.

"No, I was moved to several villages. One day, an Indian stormed up to my lodging with his knife drawn. He demanded that I be handed over to him. He was the father of an Indian that I shot when I was trying to escape capture, and he wanted to avenge his son's death. The king refused. After that, I was moved to another town to keep me safe from the relatives who wanted revenge."

"I suppose you were also treated kindly in this other town?" Archer asked.

Smith nodded. "I was feasted and treated with great courtesy there and in several other Indian towns. But I was kept under such careful guard that I expected the Indians to put me to death as soon as they were satisfied that all their questions were answered."

"Then how did you manage to escape from your Indian guards and get back to our fort?" Ratcliffe demanded. His voice grew shrill. "Master Smith, are you saying there's an Indian war party searching for you, as we speak? Should we be preparing ourselves for an attack?"

"President Ratcliffe, I don't think we have anything to fear from the Indians who held me captive. Four of them escorted me back to this area. They were very pleasant—even carried my gear for me. They packed bread sufficient for weeks of travel. When we came in sight of the fort, they politely waved good-bye and left."

Smith glanced around the room to be sure all the men were listening to his next words: "Among the Indians, Emperor Powhatan's commands are law. After I met him, Powhatan ordered his warriors to escort me back safely."

"You met Powhatan? The emperor of the Indians?" Sam blurted out. In the silent room, his words sounded like an explosion.

President Ratcliffe glared at the boy, and Sam shrank back against his master's knee.

Smith smirked, delighted by the dramatic emphasis that Sam's outburst had added to his announcement. "Yes, I met the great Powhatan," he said. "In fact, we had quite a long talk."

"What manner of man is this chieftain?" the men asked. "How is he treated by his people?"

"When I was brought before him, he was lying on mats piled ten or twelve high. He wore a cape made from raccoon pelts and several strands of shining pearls around his neck. Powhatan is lean and his skin is leathery from age. His hair and beard are gray, but his arms and chest ripple with muscles. I suppose he must be at least sixty, because he is the father and grandfather of grown men.

"When Powhatan sits in state, he is surrounded by ten of his chief men. These men sit tall and straight as statues, and they keep their eyes fixed steadily on their emperor. At least as many women also attend him. The women wear great chains of pearls, and each one has her head and shoulders painted red. Powhatan conducts himself with as much dignity as a king in a European court. He's a ruler, accustomed to command and respect."

A long pause followed Smith's description of the Indians' emperor. At last, President Ratcliffe cleared his throat and caught the eye of Gabriel Archer. "Master Smith," Ratcliffe began, "as extraordinary as your experiences were, they do not absolve you of responsibility."

Sam sat up, gaping at Ratcliffe. He turned and looked at his master.

"My responsibility?" Smith exclaimed. "What are you saying, Ratcliffe? Speak plain!"

Ratcliffe's nostrils flared and he pursed his lips. "What I am saying, Master Smith, is that three of our men were ambushed and put to death by savages while under your command. And now you come back to the fort, pleased with yourself and telling us tales of the savages' dignity and courtesy." Ratcliffe's voice rose. "Those men were your responsibility, John Smith," he thundered, "Their deaths are your responsibility!"

Smith's jaw fell, and he stared openmouthed at the president.

"I am removing you from the council, Master Smith, because you are not fit to lead other men. As for your punishment—"

"Punishment!" Smith roared, jumping to his feet. "Punishment? I spent a month as the prisoner of savages who are more civilized than my own people, it seems. Now I am come back to English justice, and I am stripped of my rightful place on the council without a trial. And you have the gall to speak of punishment! How dare you...."

Reverend Hunt stood and strode across the room. He put a hand on Smith's shoulder and turned to face Ratcliffe. "If there are accusations against John Smith, then we must investigate the evidence and proceed according to the laws of England. Surely, any thoughts of punishment are premature before the charges are examined, Mister President."

Ratcliffe rose and pointed at the doorway. "If you will step outside, Master Smith. The council will consider this matter immediately and—"

"May I remind you that I am still a member of this council, Ratcliffe!" Smith shouted.

"During your extended absence, Smith," Ratcliffe said in a voice that trembled with anger, "the council appointed Gabriel Archer to replace you."

"Under what system of law shall a man be replaced by another before he has even been removed from office?" Smith demanded.

Most of the councilmen were on their feet by now, and the

room shook with angry voices. In the midst of the hubbub, one of the guards charged into the room wearing his helmet and breastplate. "Begging your pardon, gentlemen," he announced breathlessly. "A sailing ship has been sighted on the river. It looks like an English ship."

The men stopped shouting and poured out of Ratcliffe's house. By the time they reached the southern guard platform, the guards were cheering.

"It's Cap'n Newport!" one guard yelled. "He's returned!"

Fire!

Aship was slowly making its way toward the bank. Sam could see English sailors on deck, gathering in the sails and tying them down. Finally, the ship lay at anchor, bobbing gently beside the shore.

Clapping and cheering, the settlers gathered around Captain Newport, who had just stepped ashore. Smiling triumphantly, he began shaking hands with the gentlemen. "Are the others in the fort?" he asked.

"The others are dead," said one of the men. "This is all we have left—barely forty men, Cap'n."

Newport's smile vanished. His eyes scanned the group standing around him. "Are you saying that more than half of our settlers died?"

The colonists nodded sadly. Sam remembered the summer day almost six months ago, when they had assembled on this riverbank to shout farewell to Captain Newport before he sailed for England. Sam realized how pathetic this small group of ragged men must look to Newport.

Newport stared. "President Wingfield?" he asked, searching for the face of the man he had left in charge.

John Ratcliffe stepped forward instead. "Master Wingfield is no longer our president, Captain. He was found guilty of hoarding supplies and suspected of cooperating with a spy. He is under guard aboard the *Discovery*. I'm the president of the council now."

Newport absorbed this news. "You say there was a spy? Here, in our colony?"

Ratcliffe nodded, his face reddening. Sam knew that Ratcliffe had been close friends with George Kendall in the weeks before the treachery was discovered. He suspected that Ratcliffe would have liked to avoid discussing the Kendall matter.

John Smith, on the other hand, was delighted to tell Newport about Kendall's treachery. "Yes, Captain," he said, pushing his way through the crowd. "We caught George Kendall stealing a ship loaded with supplies. As soon as we tried him, we executed the blackguard!"

"My word! So George Kendall was a Spanish spy!" Newport exclaimed, shaking his head. "And Captain Ratcliffe is now president of the council. What about Bartholomew Gosnold? Where is he?"

"Captain Gosnold died of the—" Smith began.

Ratcliffe rushed in. "Captain Gosnold died of the sickness," he said, glaring at Smith. As the colony's president, Ratcliffe felt he should be the one to deliver the report to Captain Newport. "A terrible sickness has claimed the lives of scores of our men."

"One sickness took the lives of more than fifty men?" Newport asked, astonished.

"Our men were weakened from lack of food," Ratcliffe explained. "But not all the deaths were caused by sickness. Many died of wounds inflicted by the savages. Although we have engaged the savages in trade during the months since we last saw you, Captain Newport, they cannot be trusted. They have repeatedly demonstrated their cunning, murderous natures.

"And some of the blame must fall on our leaders, I regret to say," Ratcliffe continued. "There are those amongst us who have been reckless in dealing with the savages. Why, just last month, irresponsible leadership during a trading party cost the lives of three of our men." Pausing to catch his breath, Ratcliffe scowled at John Smith.

Sam watched his master's eyes narrow. He expected the shouting match from the council meeting to resume.

But Captain Newport's attention had strayed, his gaze wandering through the crowd. "William Brewster is dead?" he asked. "And Master Edward's young kinsman, Stephen Calthrop? What of John Robinson?" he asked. "And Eustace Clovell? All dead?"

As he recited each name, the survivors nodded sadly. "I had no idea how difficult the conditions were here in Virginia," Newport said. The captain's voice took on a more encouraging tone. "But I've brought a ship laden with supplies. And eighty Englishmen are aboard who've come to join the colony. Another forty men and more provisions are following on my companion ship, the *Phoenix*. She was close behind me until we lost sight of her in a cloud bank yesterday." Newport looked from man to man. "Consider your ordeal at an end, my friends!"

The men cheered. Some of the laborers smiled and slapped their neighbor's backs. Tears streamed down the cheeks of a few gentlemen as they clasped Captain Newport's hands.

Sam clapped a hand on Nate's shoulder, "You heard Captain Newport—our ordeal is over! We've got to stop looking behind us now, Nate. We survived the seasoning, and we've got our future ahead of us. All of England will hear that we did what we came to do—we planted a colony in the New World!"

Nate looked at Sam, but he did not smile.

In the excitement following Newport's arrival, thoughts of punishing John Smith were set aside. Everyone was eager to have a look at the goods the sailors were unloading. A treasure trove of food and ammunition, tools and weapons, fabric and clothing was stored on Newport's ship, the *John and Francis*. In addition to the provisions, the ship had brought letters from England.

Smith sent Sam to collect his mail. A gentleman handed the boy a pile of letters for his master. "I think this one's for you, son," he said, handing Sam another letter.

Sam looked at the writing on the outside. He recognized his brother Thomas's scrawling letters. Running to deliver the mail to his master, Sam trembled with excitement. This was the first letter he'd ever received.

Thomas's letter was dated late summer. He'd written a few lines. He said their parents were healthy and often talked about what Sam's life might be like—so far from Lincolnshire. Sam's two little sisters were doing well. Anne, Sam's favorite, particularly sent her regards. Thomas reported that the farm was enjoying a good harvest, and Father did not expect them to run short. Mother wanted to know about Sam's health and if he was keeping warm and getting enough to eat. They all missed him and hoped Master Smith was kind to him.

That was all. Sam read the words over and over, trying to squeeze more information from them. Sam read the letter again by firelight, then tucked it under his bedroll. It made him feel important. He was becoming a man, old enough to leave home and receive a letter from his family. He felt proud that he could read the words himself.

But the letter also made Sam restless. He kept thinking about home—the livestock in the old barn, the fields, the loft in their cottage where he and Thomas slept. He tried to imagine how everyone looked. As he pulled his blanket up to his chin, Sam thought of his mother, and he could almost feel the gentle touch of her hand against his cheek. He remembered how the hem of her skirt would be stiff with mud when she came inside on rainy days. He could see her upper lip glistening with sweat as she worked near the hot kitchen fire. But he could not remember what her face looked like! *How could I forget what my own mother looks like?* He started to sweat under his blankets. *If Mother came to James Fort tomorrow, would I be able to pick her out of a crowd?* For a moment, Sam felt completely alone. Deep within his chest, he felt a heaviness that nearly took away his breath. Sam clenched his fists. "Quit thinking like a baby," he whispered to himself. "Of course you'd recognize your own mother!"

Lying in the dark sleeping quarters, he listened to Nate's even breathing beside him. Finally, he fell asleep.

In the morning, Captain Newport visited their lodging. He'd heard about Smith's capture by the Indians, and he wanted to hear about Smith's experiences firsthand. In particular, Newport was interested in Smith's meeting with Emperor Powhatan.

Smith repeated the description he had given to the council. He told Newport about the talks he had with the emperor. "I told Powhatan that you were our 'father' in Virginia. The emperor is eager to meet you, Captain."

"And I'm eager to meet him, as well," Newport said. "As soon as our affairs allow, Smith, I want you to take me to see this famous Powhatan."

As they rolled up the blankets and tidied the quarters, Sam and Nate listened to the men talk. The boys caught each other's eye when Newport said that he wanted Smith to take him to see the famous Indian emperor. Both boys hoped they would go along on that expedition!

"While I was in England," Newport continued. "I selected some handsome gifts for Powhatan: A white greyhound, a suit of fine red cloth, and a plumed hat—gifts that would flatter the finest European prince. I think Powhatan will be very pleased." Newport beamed.

Smith hesitated. "Captain Newport," he said slowly, "I think it's best to keep the upper hand with Powhatan. He may interpret your gifts as a form of tribute—a sign that we consider his empire mightier than our own. In my opinion, this would be a serious misjudgment of—"

"Nonsense, man!" Newport interrupted. "Do you think I've never traveled in the heathen lands? Why, the best way to keep the natives peaceful is to parade these showy trinkets before their eyes! It flatters their vanity." Newport chuckled. "Listen, Smith. For all his power, Powhatan is merely a rustic savage. When has he ever seen the likes of a snow-white greyhound? Or beheld the vivid color of our best red cloth? Why, he'll view these things as miracles! Such gifts are signs of our wealth and power. Once we establish our superiority, the man will quake before the might of England!"

Sam watched his master out of the corner of his eye. Smith started to say something, then thought better of it. With President Ratcliffe eager to blame Smith for the deaths of the men on the trading expedition, his master needed Captain Newport's goodwill. To Sam's great relief, his master held his tongue, and the two men smiled and parted as friends.

During the next few days, the guards kept a lookout for Newport's companion ship, but there was no sign of the *Phoenix*. Newport began to worry that the ship had run aground in the fog and sunk. Meanwhile, the sailors unloaded the cargo from the *John and Francis* into the fort's storehouse. They carried heavy sacks of grain and seed, and wooden barrels of flour. Boxes of shot and gunpowder were stacked from floor to ceiling inside the wooden storehouse. Smoked meats were tied to the rafters. Sam, Nate, and Richard offered to help with the heavy work of lifting and carrying, so they could see for themselves all the wonderful supplies the Virginia Company had sent to fortify the hungry colony.

Sam also helped the passengers from the *John and Francis* get settled in the fort. Until more sleeping quarters could be built, the newcomers would have to crowd in with the original settlers. The newcomers were nervous and uncomfortable in these strange new surroundings. They asked Sam questions about the climate in Virginia and what sorts of crops could be grown in the soil. Mostly, they inquired about the natives and what types of weapons they had.

When Sam tried to look at their colony from the viewpoint of these passengers, he had to smile. *We must look as thin as saplings to them, and our clothes are no better than rags! The walls of our fort probably seem sturdy enough. But inside the palisade, our buildings are no more than huts.* Sam suspected that the newcomers were amazed by how little progress seemed to have been made in Virginia. *To think that more than fifty Englishmen have already given their lives to this paltry effort!*

But things will get better now, Sam thought. *With a well-stocked storehouse and eighty new men, our settlement will soon flourish. There'll be enough hands to make our sleeping quarters snug against the chill of winter and to build more housing. When spring comes, planting will be a pleasure with so many to share the work.*

Five days after the arrival of the *John and Francis,* Sam was standing guard duty. He squinted up and down the river in hope of spotting the *Phoenix.* When his eyes began to smart from the sun's glare off the surface of the water, he turned and watched the activity in the fort.

A wisp of smoke drifted up from the center of the fort. Sam didn't think anything of it. Gray curls of smoke were an everyday sight in the sky above the fort because all the cooking was done over open fires. But something about that smoke caught Sam's attention. As he watched, the curl began to thicken. He heard a crackling noise, followed by popping. Horrified, Sam

It was hopeless—the fire had already spread.

traced the tail of smoke downward. A flame was eating through the thatched roof of the storehouse!

Instantly, Sam jumped off the platform, screaming, "Fire!"

Men came running from all directions. But the storehouse was already a roaring oven. As the settlers watched helplessly, its thatched roof blazed, and clods of burning thatch fell inside the building. Sam's only thought was their food—the smoked meats, the barrels of flour, and the rest. Almost the entire supply of the colony's food for the winter was inside that inferno!

"Water!" Sam shouted. "We need water from the river!" He grabbed a pail and dashed through the open gate.

By the time Sam reached the river, the fort sounded like it was under assault. Sharp pops, loud cracks, and great exploding bangs were coming from inside the walls. Sam turned to see flaming balls shooting into the sky. They arced and fell back into the fort. *The gunpowder!* he thought with horror. *All the gunpowder and shot are in the storehouse!*

Sam and the others frantically filled pails, pitchers, jugs—any containers they could find—and raced to the fort. But it was hopeless—the fire had already spread. Clods of burning thatch shot into the air and landed on the roofs of other wooden buildings. Consuming the thatch like kindling, the fire quickly set the buildings' walls and posts on fire. Men tore screaming through the fort, trying to grab their possessions as walls of flame leaped up on all sides of them. In the end, the colonists were forced to flee for their lives.

Settlers, both old and new, and sailors huddled outside the fort and watched the flames devour the buildings and the supplies inside them. Many of the men wept as they watched. Others ran their fingers through their hair and rocked back and forth mournfully.

Nate and Richard stood next to Sam. Soot streaked their faces. Richard had managed to grab a blanket, and he draped it around his shoulders. Its edges were charred and it was pocked with holes.

Sam looked into Nate's eyes. He knew what his friend was thinking—Nate had said it often enough: "James Fort is a place of death." Sam tried to swallow, but his mouth was dry, and he felt like a lump of ash was wedged in his throat. The smell of burnt wood filled his nose. The roar of the flames blasted his ears, and smoke stung his eyes. *James Fort is a place of death,* Sam thought. *It is the worst place imaginable.*

Above the noise of the fire, Sam heard John Smith's voice. "The palisade!" Smith was hollering. "Look! The flames are so hot that the timbers are catching fire! We've got to douse the outer walls or we'll lose the fort!" Sam edged through the crowd toward his master.

Smith took command. He ordered the men to bring barrels, jugs, kettles—anything that would hold water. Then he nudged the men into orderly lines leading from the river to the fort. Sam took a place in line beside one of the new settlers. Richard stood on his right. They worked feverishly without speaking, reserving all their energy to lift the heavy containers and pass them up the lines. For hours, Sam worked, thinking of nothing but grabbing the next container and passing it to Richard without spilling the precious water. Some of the men collapsed from exhaustion. Others filled their places in the lines. But Sam did not hear anybody grumbling about the backbreaking work. For once, the Englishmen worked as one body with a common purpose.

By nightfall, the fire had burned to embers. Although some timbers along the outer walls were badly charred, the fort would stand. Men sprawled on the frozen ground—faces blackened, bodies and minds exhausted.

Captain Newport and President Ratcliffe went to the captain's quarters on the ships to get some sleep. Smith took charge of assigning the men to sleep on the 'tween deck in shifts. While one group slept, he ordered the others to patrol the rubble and put out stray sparks.

When Sam awoke in the morning and climbed to the open deck, his heart sank. Although he had awakened during the night with the taste of ash in his throat, the fire had seemed like a bad dream. Daylight brought reality slamming into his brain. All those months of work! Now only three scorched buildings remained standing inside the walls. From the river, the fort looked like an ugly black nutshell, its jagged edges stabbing at the gray, wintry sky.

Outfoxing the Emperor

After the fire, the settlers moved about like sleepwalkers. They stared across the river with vacant eyes. All those months of misery in Virginia, and now their work was reduced to ash and rubble!

"I say it's time to give up and go back to England,"one man muttered. "We'll never survive the winter. We don't have enough food to last a month here!"

"Impossible!" another argued. "The ships aren't big enough to carry us all."

Others nodded, their hands trembling. "Even if we could squeeze everybody onto the ships, what would we eat during the crossing? We have a better chance of finding food here than we do on board a ship."

"Well, I say we're better off to take the risk of starving at sea than stay here and freeze to death. We're short of everything—clothes, blankets, tools!"

These conversations terrified Sam. As he listened to the men's predictions of slow but certain death, he felt icy prickles of fear running up and down his arms.

To drive off his panic, Sam stuck close to John Smith's side. More than ever, he admired his master's determination. Smith was at his best in a crisis. He worked tirelessly. He slept in short snatches. While Captain Newport and President Ratcliffe held meetings with the gentlemen to discuss how to organize the process of rebuilding, John Smith concerned himself with immediate tasks. He assigned cleanup crews to carry burnt rubble out of the fort, he rationed the small supply of provisions left on board the *John and Francis,* and he sent out hunting parties. *I've never seen my master hesitate,* Sam reflected. *Never heard him complain.*

A few days after the fire, the guards spotted a small boat approaching the fort. Sam followed Smith onto the platform and looked in the direction the guards were pointing. A single canoe was making its way up the James River. Sam squinted. "Indians. And most of them are young women!" he exclaimed. He shaded his eyes with his hands. "I see two men in the canoe. The other three are Indian girls, Master Smith."

Smith smiled as the canoe pulled close to the shore. "That's Powhatan's daughter," he said. Jumping off the platform, he walked briskly to the riverbank.

Sam ran to catch up. "You know Powhatan's daughter?" he asked. He wondered why Smith hadn't mentioned the girl when he related his experiences as the Indians' prisoner.

Smith nodded. "Her name is Pocahontas," he said. "My life belongs to her."

Astonished, Sam gaped at his master. Smith was already hurrying toward the canoe. Curious, Sam jogged behind.

Three Indian girls sat in the canoe, clasping animal furs around their shoulders. The hair over the top and sides of their heads was cut to a stubble, but in the back, it hung in a long, glossy black braid. Sam had seen this hairstyle on unmarried girls in the Indian villages during their trading expeditions.

Two of the girls, who looked about Sam's age, pushed aside the hides and got out of the canoe. Wading through the cold water, they pulled their boat onto the shore. The men stayed in the boat, their faces stern as they watched Sam and Smith. The smallest girl stepped onto the shore. Sam thought she looked about eleven, the same age as his sister, Anne.

Smith clasped the girl's hand in both of his. He nodded his head and said, "Welcome to Jamestown, Pocahontas." Smith gestured at the gate to the fort.

Pocahontas studied the walls of the fort, shielding her eyes against the sun to gaze at the tops of the charred palisade.

"Would you like to see what's left of our fort?" Smith asked, and motioned for her to follow him toward the gate.

Pocahontas smiled, but shook her head. Sam studied her face. Her deep brown eyes sparkled, and her skin was even and smooth. Like Anne, she stood a head shorter than Sam. *But she's not as slender as Anne,* he thought. *The muscles in her arms and legs look strong. And she's not timid like the other Indian girls I've seen.* Sam smiled to himself. *This is the daughter of mighty Powhatan—the emperor who commands thousands of Indians in Virginia!*

As Pocahontas spoke to Smith, she gestured with her hands. Sam couldn't understand her words, but he was sure he heard her say the name Powhatan. But Smith nodded as if he understood. Then Pocahontas turned and spoke to her companions. The other girls picked up great baskets of food and unloaded them onto the shore, then carried a pile of furry skins out of the canoe and laid them on the ground.

As soon as they set the presents down, Pocahontas and the other girls got back into the canoe. Sam helped Smith push their boat into the water. As Sam released the canoe, Pocahontas looked him in the eye and smiled. Sam lowered his eyes and felt his cheeks grow hot. He was suddenly embarrassed to be wearing such filthy, torn clothing. He stood beside Smith and waved at the canoe as the girls paddled into the middle of the river.

"That girl who spoke to you," Sam said, hoping to spark a conversation, "Pocahontas. She's the daughter of Powhatan?"

Smith nodded. He picked up two of the baskets and headed toward the fort.

"Why did you say your life belongs to her?" Sam asked, as he lifted one of the baskets.

"It's a long story," Smith answered, as he strode to the fort to find Captain Newport.

~

Without shelters inside the fort, the colonists had to sleep aboard the ships. That night, Sam wrapped his blanket around him and huddled on deck to wait for his master. The others had gone below where it would be warmer. As soon as Smith came aboard, Sam sat up.

Grinning, Smith said, "I figured you'd be too curious to sleep, Sam Collier!" He leaned against the ship's rail, and waited for Sam to join him.

Sam edged closer so they could speak quietly.

"As I told you," Smith began, "the girl's name is Pocahontas, and she's one of the daughters of the Emperor Powhatan." Although they were alone on deck, Smith spoke softly, so the sound wouldn't carry to the sleepers on the 'tween deck below. "Judging by the way the old ruler treats her, I'd guess she's a favorite. As soon as the Indians took me to Powhatan's court, I noticed her.

"She's a lively girl, full of curiosity about our English ways. One afternoon, when I was living in Powhatan's village, I set my coat down as I talked with an old brave. When I turned around, I realized that Pocahontas had crept up close to me. She was fingering the fabric and examining the stitches. Before she realized I was watching her, I saw her test the strength of the buttons with her teeth! Another time, I left my shoes by the edge of the river while I waded into the water to watch some Indians fish. When I looked back at the bank, I saw her slipping her feet into my shoes. She actually tried to walk in them."

"Why did you say that your life belongs to her?" Sam asked. Remembering Smith's stories about his captivity in Turkey, Sam added, "Are you her slave?"

"No," Smith said thoughtfully, "she doesn't own me as a master owns a slave. This is more of a ceremonial arrangement. When I was taken before Powhatan, the great ruler asked me many questions," Smith continued. "A feast was spread before me. I ate, then two braves lugged heavy stones to the side of the fire and set them down so the edges touched to form a sort of flat-topped altar. Suddenly, many Indians surrounded me, dragged me to the fire, and forced me to lay my head on the stones. They held clubs above their heads and ran at me." Smith paused for a moment. "I closed my eyes and made my peace with God, because I was sure they were going to bash my head in."

Sam gasped. "Did they beat you?"

"No," Smith said. "As soon as I closed my eyes, I felt small hands gently stroking my face. I opened my eyes, and that child, Pocahontas, was bending over me. She stood up and faced Powhatan. When she spoke, her voice was without expression—it reminded me of the way a child might repeat a memorized poem. Powhatan answered, and his voice was deep and rhythmic, as if he was reciting the words of a ceremony. After he spoke, his braves backed away, and Pocahontas helped me to my feet.

"After that, the child visited my lodging and brought me presents of food and skins. I asked the guard what it all meant. He laughed and said my life belonged to Pocahontas. The guard seemed to think it was a grand joke—Powhatan had given my life to a child. And a mere girl, at that."

As Sam tried to picture Powhatan's ceremony, his mind kept flashing back to the clearing in the Apokant village, where he had witnessed the torture of George Cassen. He remembered how Cassen had screamed and begged. *I wonder if Powhatan expected my master to scream when the braves dragged him to the fire.* Sam couldn't imagine his master begging for his life.

"You never spoke of this before," Sam said. He dropped his voice to a whisper. "Why didn't you tell the council members about Pocahontas?"

"There was no need," Smith said. "I'm the only Englishman who has actually seen and spoken to the mighty Emperor Powhatan. This gives me a powerful advantage. If I told the council about this ceremony, Ratcliffe and the others might think the Indians belittled me. I told the council as much as they need to know and no more."

Sam was puzzled. "But what if the council discovers that you lied...."

"I never lie, Sam," Smith said. "Neither do I engage in useless conversation. A wise man chooses to tell that portion of the truth that serves his purpose."

Sam looked at the black sky dotted with tiny, glimmering lights and considered John Smith's words. *George Kendall, the spy, also told only that portion of the truth that served his purpose,* Sam thought. *Kendall admitted as little as he could to avoid being prosecuted for treason. But when a man is innocent, doesn't he share the whole truth?*

Smith put a hand on the boy's shoulder. "Enough stories for one night, Sam." Smith walked to the ship's ladder. Before he climbed down, he added, "Time to sleep now."

Sam remembered Nate saying that Master Smith was a hard man to like. Tonight, Sam felt the same way. He waited until he could no longer hear Smith's footsteps, then he went below and found a spot between the sleeping bodies to spread open his blanket. He lay awake, his mind buzzing, and he wished he could talk to Nate about what Smith had told him. But he knew his master had trusted him with a kind of secret. Although he wasn't sure if he agreed with John Smith that a wise man should choose to tell only part of the truth, Sam was very sure that a wise man does not betray other people's secrets.

⁓

Almost eighty healthy new settlers had arrived on the *John and Francis.* They were evenly divided between laborers and gentlemen. With so many new hands, rebuilding the fort went much faster than Sam expected. A makeshift storehouse was put up in a few days, and work was started on new sleeping quarters. In a few weeks, the burnt timbers in the fort's walls were replaced, and the settlement looked almost the same as it did before the fire.

Once or twice a week, Indians came to the fort. Sometimes Pocahontas returned, and other times Indian men came. They brought presents of bread and dried corn, deer or raccoon meat. The messengers always approached the gate and waited until the guards located John Smith. Smith was the only Englishman that the Indians ever asked to see.

Smith greeted both the Indian girls and men outside the gate. All of the messengers recited a short speech from Powhatan, which included greetings and an invitation for Smith to visit. The messengers reminded Smith that Powhatan wanted to meet the colony's "father," Captain Newport. Sometimes the Indians came inside the fort with Smith to view the Englishmen's strange dwellings.

Sam wondered if President Ratcliffe or the other gentlemen resented the way the Indians treated John Smith—as if Smith was the man in charge. Of course, none of the Englishmen would dare to voice a complaint because they needed the Indians' food and goodwill.

In early February, Captain Newport decided to make the long-awaited visit to Powhatan. Since John Smith had shown his skill in dealing with the natives, the captain put him in charge of arrangements. Smith chose Sam and about forty strong men to go along. He ordered the men to pack armor, helmets, weapons, and ammunition, as well as food. He also had them load a large pile of the trade goods that Newport had brought from England.

With Smith as guide, the shallop traveled down the James River, into Chesapeake Bay, and north to the Pamunkey River, which ran parallel to the James. About twenty miles up the Pamunkey, Smith said he recognized the countryside around Powhatan's town, Werowocomoco. Smith took Sam and nineteen men in light armor to locate the town. Captain Newport and the others waited on the boat.

Like the men, Sam wore an iron helmet and a jack, a quilted jacket made of linen with plates of iron sewn inside. Although the jack was heavy and didn't offer as much protection from arrows as an iron breastplate, Sam liked wearing it better because it wasn't as stiff.

They marched into the woods, where they met a band of Indian men. Smith greeted the leader, a son of Powhatan, and called him by name. Then Smith ordered his men to follow the Indians. Winding along trails through the woods, they reached a creek. On the far side was Werowocomoco. Sam could see many reed dwellings in the town. Women squatted by fires and clusters of children played nearby.

Powhatan's son indicated a wooden footbridge across the creek and invited Smith to lead his men across. The flimsy bridge was built on forked stakes pounded into the mud. Poles had been laid across the stakes and lashed in place with vines.

Sam wondered how many men the bridge could hold without collapsing. The Englishmen wore heavy iron jacks and helmets and carried weapons, so they weighed a lot more than the Indians. Sam glanced down at the icy water moving swiftly in the creek, and he winced. *If the bridge gives way and I fall in, I'll sink with this heavy armor on,* Sam thought. He looked at John Smith, who was talking with Powhatan's son. *Does my master see the danger?*

Smith kept talking with Powhatan's son as he positioned Sam and nine men as guards at the entrance to the bridge. He mingled the remaining Englishmen among the Indians. Then, Smith approached the bridge and stepped fearlessly onto the wobbly planks. Since Powhatan's son was in the middle of a conversation, he could not hesitate without showing his fear, so he stepped boldly onto the footbridge, too. The wooden stakes jiggled and jerked. As the mingled group of Indians and Englishmen began to follow their leaders, the rickety bridge creaked and sagged.

Powhatan's son glanced behind him at the group on the bridge and stopped. He waved at some Indians on the opposite shore, who pushed a large canoe into the water and paddled to the bridge. All the Englishmen and the Indians clambered off the bridge and into the boat. When they reached the village, Powhatan's son urged Smith to hurry and visit his father. But Smith politely insisted on waiting until the rest of his men were safely across the creek.

Sam had learned to read John Smith's thoughts in the set of his jaw. He knew his master was angry, and he thought he understood why. *The rickety bridge was a way to test my master's courage and cunning. John Smith passed this test by thinking quickly.* Sam felt a chill in the air. *What other tests does Emperor Powhatan have in store for us?*

Smith lined his men up two by two behind him. After he gave the command to march, he looked at Sam and said, "Look to your back, lad! Warn the others."

Sam nodded and whispered to the man beside him. "Watch out. Our commander doesn't trust these Indians." As the Englishmen marched into Werowocomoco, they passed Smith's warning down the line.

When they came to a large dwelling in the center of the town, Smith ordered his men to halt. "This is Emperor Powhatan's lodge," Smith announced. He told the men to stand guard while he ducked into the entrance.

After several minutes, Smith returned. He was holding a roasted deer leg in his hand. "Powhatan has invited us to come inside to eat."

The soldiers moved forward.

"Wait!" Smith looked at his men. "We will enjoy Powhatan's hospitality, but we will put caution ahead of comfort. Enter the lodge two at a time. The others will remain at attention outside." Smith motioned for two gentlemen to enter the lodge. Since Sam was up front near his master, Smith told him to go in with the gentlemen.

Powhatan's lodge looked just like the other Indian homes that Sam had seen, except it was much larger and it was covered with sheets of bark rather than woven reeds. The walls of the lodge were supported by a framework of saplings lashed together. It took a few seconds for Sam's eyes to get used to the dim, hazy light of torches. Many people were seated inside, some on wide benches against the walls, some on the ground.

Sam immediately began to sweat because the lodge was so warm. In the center, a hole had been dug in the dirt floor and lined with stones for a fireplace. Although most of the smoke escaped through an opening in the roof, the lodge smelled smoky.

An older man was seated near the fire, with others on each side of him. By the man's bearing, Sam knew at once that this was the Emperor Powhatan. After hearing so many stories about this mighty leader, Sam had expected a huge hulk of a man with stout limbs and a scowling face. Instead, he saw a slim grandfather with twinkling eyes. A cape of raccoon skins was draped over his shoulders, the striped tails dangling over his chest. Like his braves, he wore a piece of tanned deerskin around his waist. Deerskin leggings covered his legs from his thighs to his ankles. The right side of his head was shaved, but on the left side his thin, gray hair was gathered into a knot and decorated with a ring of red-dyed deer fur. Thick strands of pearl circled his neck and glistened on his chest. Dangling from his earlobes were tiny bird claws holding loops of copper wire.

As Sam sat down behind the gentlemen, Powhatan studied the boy's face. Sam lowered his eyes respectfully. The Indian emperor spoke sharply, his tone ringing like a command.

Sam stiffened and met Powhatan's gaze.

Leaning forward, Powhatan raised his bushy white eyebrows. Sam was sure the emperor was talking to him, and he looked nervously around the lodge, searching the faces of the other Indians for an explanation of what he was supposed to do.

Powhatan was surrounded by his warriors. Most of them were unclothed except for the piece of leather around their waists. Their naked bodies glistened as if they had coated them-selves with oil. The warriors stared at Sam, their faces unmoving.

Behind the men stood women, with faces painted red and milky-white strands of pearls around their necks. Sam recognized Pocahontas sitting with other children in a corner of the lodge. When his eyes met hers, she smiled and held up her hands to indicate Sam's gun.

Confused, Sam looked at his weapon. Powhatan repeated his command.

Sam knew at once that this was the Emperor Powhatan.

Suddenly Smith brushed past Sam and spoke in an angry tone. "No! My men keep their weapons. It is not our custom to lay our guns at the feet of a foreign king. Only an enemy would make such a request. Never a friend!"

Sam glanced quickly from his master's face to Powhatan's. John Smith stared at the emperor, his jaw as firm as iron.

Powhatan shrugged. Two women quickly came forward and handed Sam and the English gentlemen several cakes of bread. As soon as his men took the bread, Smith ordered them to leave and send two more men inside.

That night, their group camped in Werowocomoco. Smith ordered a double guard and refused to let the men wander around the town. In the morning, after the group returned to the shallop, an Indian messenger paddled out to them with an invitation from Powhatan. Smith nodded as the messenger spoke. "The Indians are inviting us to trade with them."

The messenger pointed at Smith's gun and said a few more words. He was telling the Englishmen to leave their weapons and armor behind when they returned to Werowocomoco. He also told Smith to be sure and bring the white father, Captain Newport, because Powhatan wished to meet and honor him.

In spite of these instructions, Smith ordered his men to wear their jacks and helmets and carry their guns when they returned to Powhatan's town. This time, Captain Newport accompanied the group. One sailor carried a box containing the presents for Powhatan. Another sailor led the white greyhound on a leash. Several men carried boxes of trade goods.

When Powhatan met the Englishmen at the entrance to his lodge, he invited them to leave their weapons outside. But Smith refused politely, then introduced Captain Newport. Powhatan made a little speech, and Newport presented his gifts.

Powhatan beamed when he saw the greyhound. Running his leathery hands over the back and legs of the dog, he exclaimed over the animal's snow-white fur. At a signal from Newport, the sailor sprinted around the clearing with the dog bounding alongside him. The emperor clapped his hands to show his pleasure.

Captain Newport handed Powhatan the red suit and plumed hat. Unfolding the clothing, Powhatan rubbed it against his face to feel its softness. He put the fancy plumed hat on his head and led the Englishmen into his lodge.

Inside, Powhatan spoke and Smith translated. "He says you're a powerful leader of a mighty people, Captain Newport. He is honored to be visited by such a great commander."

Powhatan continued speaking, but Smith fell silent. Pausing, the emperor frowned at Smith. When Powhatan resumed his speech, his voice was insistent. "Now he is saying that you are too important to trade like a common man, Captain," Smith said. "So he's offering to spread out his trading goods for you to inspect, and he invites you to do the same. Since you're the guest, he wants you to have the honor of beginning this ceremony. But I don't think you should—"

Newport's face was flushed with pleasure, and he waved Smith aside. "I told you he'd be charmed by our presents, John. Of course we'll spread out our trade goods. It would be demeaning to bicker like street peddlers." Newport motioned for the sailors to open the boxes and spread out the trade goods. Along with hatchets and other iron tools, the sailors placed twelve shiny copper cooking pots on the mats.

Smith started to object, then swallowed his words. After the English goods were displayed, Powhatan signaled his braves to bring in baskets of corn and grain. Spread over the mats, the food looked plentiful. But Sam had seen his master trade a few hatchets for much more. Just one of the copper pots was worth that much food!

Newport nodded vigorously to show that the offer pleased him, and Powhatan signaled his men to carry away all the English trade goods. Smith watched in silence.

Afterward, during the meal, Smith pulled out a handful of blue glass beads and showed one of Powhatan's sons how they sparkled in the firelight. The brave asked if he could hold the beads. Smith nodded, and the brave took them to Powhatan, who shrugged as if the beads were no more interesting than pebbles. But in a few minutes, the brave brought two bearskins to Smith and offered to trade them for the handful of beads.

Smith looked shocked. He refused and held out his hand for the beads. The brave hesitated, then called to one of the women. She brought another bearskin and a basket of dried corn.

Again Smith shook his head. When the brave added more baskets of corn to the pile, Smith reluctantly agreed to the trade.

Sam kept his eyes on the ground and forced himself not to grin. *My master is every bit as cunning as the great Emperor Powhatan!* he thought.

As the Englishmen stood to leave, the brave offered to trade more food for more of the sparkling beads. Smith held out his empty hands to show he didn't have any more beads with him. The brave added a tanned hide to his offer, but Smith shrugged. "The beads are very rare and precious," he explained. "They are like pieces of blue sky," he said and waved his hand toward the heavens. Smith turned to leave, and the brave doubled his offer.

Just before he ducked out of the lodge, Smith said he would search the shallop. "Perhaps I can find a few more beads in one of the chests."

Like Sam, the other Englishmen watched this exchange without comment. But as soon as they left Powhatan's lodge, the smirks on the faces of the sailors were as loud as any cheer they might have given Smith for outfoxing Powhatan!

Before the shallop returned to James Fort, Smith bargained a pouch of cheap blue glass beads for a boatload of food and furs. Sam never heard Smith say anything to Captain Newport about squandering precious copper pots on a mere handful of grain. And Newport did not mention all the food and furs that they were bringing back to the fort. But Sam suspected the two men were communicating through their silence.

Jamestown

The winter of 1608 was bitterly cold, but Sam was too busy to complain. During the months of February and March, sailors and settlers worked side by side. They tramped across frosty ground in search of trees to build more housing. They split cedar into clapboard to fill the hold of the *John and Francis* with products to sell in England. They sailed the shallop up and down the river in search of gold, and they traded with Indians for dried corn and furs. Since game was scarce and lean in winter, hunters ranged for miles in search of deer, rabbits, and squirrels. Inside the fort, the men tanned hides, hung strips of meat to dry, sewed crude footwear from deerskin, and made nets to catch fish. When the ground began to warm, they prepared fields for spring planting.

Sam, Nate, and Richard were assigned chores in and around the fort. One afternoon, they were at work on the riverbank, splitting the trunk of a cedar into clapboard and loading the rough boards onto the *John and Francis*. It was a crisp afternoon, and the sun was clear and bright. After the boys finished their work, one of the gentlemen sent them to gather dead twigs for kindling.

The ground around the fort had been picked clean, so the boys had to walk a fair distance into the woods. They passed a group of hunters. "Out for a stroll, lads?" one of them said, smiling through his bushy beard.

Sam grinned. "We're hunting, too—hunting for kindling!" he joked.

"Hope your hunt is as successful as ours," said one of the men. He was holding one end of a thick branch from which hung a deer carcass.

The hunter holding the other end of the branch said, "Better not stay out too much longer, lads. You don't want to be in the woods after dark."

The hunters tramped on. As their voices faded into the distance, Sam heard one of them say, "I recognized Peacock and young Collier. But who's the other boy?"

The men were now so far away that the boys could hardly hear them, but Sam was able to make out the answer: "That's Richard Mutton. He came here with the spy, George Kendall. What a blackguard that Kendall was! Did you hear about that? They executed him for stealing a ship."

Sam glanced at Richard to see if he'd heard the man's remarks. Richard's face was bright red, and he kicked the ground angrily.

"See that big oak?" Sam said quickly. "Last one to reach it has to carry a double load of kindling!"

Sam and Nate sprinted for the tree, but Richard hung back. "Wait," he snarled. "Let's make it a real race."

The two boys stopped running and looked at Richard. "All right," Nate said. "We'll run two at a time. First round it's you against Sam." Sam and Richard scratched a line in the dirt and put their toes on it. "Ready," Nate called. "Go!" The two boys leaped forward. Sam considered himself a speedy runner, but Richard's height gave him an advantage, and he tagged the tree an arm's length ahead of Sam.

"Okay," Richard called, breathing hard. "Now you two go."

Sam rested his hands on his knees and caught his breath. He

had never been able to outrun Nate, whose legs were as long as a grasshopper's, but he always gave it a fair try. This time, Sam managed to slap the oak a few seconds behind Nate.

Nate and Richard walked back to the starting place. They crouched, ready to race.

Suddenly Richard stood up and said, "Hold on. What does the winner get?"

Nate snorted. "There's not much to offer here in James Fort, Richard. What do you want?"

"How about a favor?" Richard asked. "Any favor within reason."

Sam and Nate looked at each other, their eyebrows raised. "Agreed," Sam called. "As long as it's reasonable." Sam called a start to the race, and Richard slammed himself forward with the speed of a cannonball. He tagged the trunk before Nate had gotten his full stride.

"Good race, Richard!" Sam cried.

As soon as he stopped panting, Nate said. "Well, Richard, you won, fair and square. What's the favor you're asking?"

Sam was expecting Richard to ask them to take his turn at guard duty or some other chore. Instead, Richard looked at Sam and said, "I want you to talk to Master Smith for me."

Sam looked puzzled. "About what?"

"I want Captain Newport to hire me as part of his crew."

"Part of his crew?" Sam was stunned. "But you'd have to leave Virginia!"

"That's right," Richard said. "Next time somebody asks who Richard Mutton is, I want the answer to be, 'He's a sailor.' After I leave this place, nobody will say that I'm the boy who worked for the Spanish spy."

"But...." Sam turned to Nate for help. "New settlers will be coming here. They'll—"

"They'll ask who I am," Richard interrupted. "And they'll be told. Just like that hunter was told."

Nate looked at Richard. "He won fair and square, Sam," Nate said. "And we promised him any favor within reason."

Sam spoke to John Smith as soon as he got a chance.

At first, Smith didn't like the idea. "Richard's already sixteen. He's big and strong enough to take a man's job here in James Fort," Smith said. "We need all the able-bodied workers we can get in Virginia." Smith looked at Sam and continued. "I know it's hard on him now, Sam. The reputation of the master rubs off on the boy, just as the father's reputation rubs off on the son. But boys grow up. When they're men, they earn their own reputation."

"Like you've earned your own reputation in Virginia?" Sam asked.

Smith nodded. "Exactly, Sam."

"And like you earned your reputation when you fought for the Dutch against the Turks?"

Smith nodded again. He knew the boy's questions were leading somewhere.

"You told me that, as a lad, you were sent to learn a merchant's trade." Sam said. "But you didn't like the life of a merchant, so you chose another way to earn your reputation as a man."

"I see your point," Smith said. "You think a lad needs to make his own choice about what he'll do as a man." He smiled. "You win, Sam Collier," he said. "You have a clever head on your shoulders. I'll speak to Captain Newport for your friend."

Newport had already noticed young Richard's strength, and he was glad to take him as part of the crew for the crossing to England. Newport was readying the *John and Francis* to leave for England in a few weeks, at the beginning of April.

The news of Newport's upcoming departure was a relief to John Smith, because the sailors were eating more of the fort's provisions than they produced. As the crew got the ship ready for the voyage, Smith and some of the gentlemen hurried to write letters to family, friends, and sponsors at home.

Sam asked John Smith if he might write a letter to his family in Lincolnshire. "That letter from my brother Thomas—it was the first letter I ever got," Sam explained. "I'd like to try my hand at writing a letter home. My family will be relieved to hear that I'm well."

Smith agreed and gave Sam paper, pen, and ink. "But take care how you word your letter, Sam. The company doesn't want us sending letters to England that might discourage others from coming over."

Sam spent a long time considering what he should write. Paper and ink were scarce, and he couldn't afford to make mistakes. When he sat down to his task, he went slowly and carefully, using his very best handwriting to show that he had not forgotten his letters.

My respected and honored father,

Our ship arrived here in May. We found Virginia very beautiful, with goodly trees, abundance of game, and wide rivers. Although winter is as cold as England, I live in a house and get enough to eat. Tell mother not to worry. The hot months were hard on us, but I survived the seasoning. Our fort's walls are sturdy now, and Master Smith has taught me to fire the guns, so I stand guard with the men.

Master Smith is very kind to me. He desires me to learn the natives' speech and has me study the building of our houses, the tending of our crops, and other skills as will prove useful to a man of this settlement.

Although I have no family on these shores, I am not entirely alone as I have a good friend called Nathaniel Peacock who is as a brother to me in Virginia. I am praying God may protect you, though I don't know when I shall see you anymore.

I remain your loving and devoted son,

Samuel Collier

Sam labored over the letter until the light was beginning to fade. Finished at last, he was very pleased with himself. He gave the letter to Master Smith, who sealed it for him. Smith had a stack of papers to send to England.

The *John and Francis* was ready to set sail on April 10, 1608. Sam and Nate shook hands with Richard on the shore, just before he boarded the ship. Richard sparred playfully with them, his freckled face grinning happily. "Perhaps I'll be on the crew of one of the supply ships coming to Virginia," he said.

"Godspeed, Richard," Sam said. "I hope a sailor's life suits you. You earned it fair and square!"

Ten days later, the fort's guards sighted a large ship coming up the James from the bay. "Ship heading this way!" they shouted. "Large ship under sail toward us! Take arms!"

Men rushed out of buildings, grabbing for their weapons.

"What colors does it fly? Is it Spanish?" voices shouted. Men leaped onto the platforms and readied the cannons for battle.

Suddenly, one of the guards called, "Hold your fire! That's the flag of England."

Another man shaded his eyes with his hand. "Why, bless my stars," he gasped. "That's the *Phoenix!*"

"The *Phoenix?* Cap'n Newport's companion ship? I thought

she was shipwrecked months ago. I figured all her men were at the bottom of the sea!"

All over the fort, the men buzzed with excitement. "Fancy that—the *Phoenix* has arrived! She's been missing for how long now?"

"Three months! It's been three months since Cap'n Newport lost sight of her in a fog. Wouldn't the Cap'n marvel to hear this?"

Sam and the settlers rushed to the riverbank to welcome Captain Nelson, his sailors, and the forty passengers on board.

"Where have you been all this time?" President Ratcliffe asked, shaking the captain's hand. "We'd given up looking for you. What happened?"

"We lost sight of the *John and Francis* in heavy fog," Captain Nelson explained. "When we couldn't find her, I assumed we'd sailed right past her on the river, so I changed direction. The fog was so thick that we lost our bearings. We hit rough weather and took some damage to the hull. By that time, we were in open waters, so I judged our best course was to head for the islands. We finally made landfall in the West Indies. As soon as I was sure the *Phoenix* was fit to sail, and the winds were with us, I retraced our course through the Chesapeake."

Even more amazing than the arrival of the *Phoenix* was what she had on board. Most of the ship's provisions were still packed in her hold. The crew and passengers had been living on what they were able to find on the islands.

Since Captain Newport would be carrying news of the disappearance of the *Phoenix* to England, Captain Nelson was eager to return and let friends and family know that his crew and passengers were safe. So the *Phoenix* remained in James Fort less than a month—just long enough to unload supplies and passengers and fill the hold with cedar wood to sell in

England. Then she sailed, leaving the English population in Virginia at more than one hundred and fifty.

~

By the time the *Phoenix* sailed for England, the days were getting hot and sticky again. Within a few weeks, some of the new settlers began to complain of stomach cramps and fevers. Sam recognized the beginnings of the sickness he and so many others had had the previous summer. Soon, the sick men were lying in their sleeping quarters, groaning with pain and delirious with fever.

"This is their seasoning, isn't it?" Sam said to John Smith, as they walked to their lodging one evening. Passing by the sleeping quarters, Sam could hear the muffled cries of the ailing men. "Do you think these men will die from the sickness?"

Smith nodded. "Some will, Sam. But we have more food and better shelter now. I don't think their seasoning will be as severe as ours."

Sam remembered the deaths of James Brumfield, Master Calthrop, and the others. "I didn't know we'd have so much sickness and death during our first year here," he said.

"It was a hard first year, Sam, but think of what we've created. We've colonized a bountiful land—a place teeming with game and fish and trees. We've planted civilization in a new world! This undertaking is certainly worth the price."

"Before we came, did you realize that so many would die?"

Smith paused. "I suspected as much. Virginia is a test for us, Sam. It tests our courage, our cunning, our determination. Only the strongest and smartest will survive. Before we started this adventure, I realized there were risks. Grave risks. But I was confident that I'd withstand the test. And I chose you as my servant boy because you have what it takes to survive."

Sam thought over his master's words. *James Brumfield wasn't strong*, he thought, *or brave. Although he was a clever boy, he had no desire to explore a new world. But others who died weren't timid and sickly like James. Some of them were brave and determined, too. Like Master Calthrop.* Sam wondered whether a man's survival really had more to do with luck than skill or strength.

~

That summer, John Smith led two expeditions to explore Chesapeake Bay and took Sam and Nate along. Smith was searching for a waterway across the continent to the South Sea. If such a passage existed, it would be a shortcut for English ships to reach the Orient, with its thriving spice and silk trade. Smith was also hoping to find deposits of minerals, especially gold. But he found neither the passage nor the minerals.

By the time the explorers returned, the colony was in turmoil. While they were gone, conditions in the fort had grown worse. Heat and sickness had caused old jealousies to flare up. Complaints and rumors about President Ratcliffe swirled around the settlement. The council removed Ratcliffe from office, and in September, John Smith was elected president.

Sam was astounded. "This is a new world for sure!" he exclaimed. "When we first came to Virginia, the other settlers didn't even want my master to serve on the council. Remember, Nate? They said he wasn't born to lead. They insisted that only men from the finest families are fit for leadership."

"I remember that some of the passengers wanted to hang your master for mutiny during the crossing. Now he's our president!" Nate said. "I wish Master Calthrop was alive to see this. He always said your master had bold ideas."

"Master John Smith—president of the Virginia colony!" Sam said, his eyes sparkling as he tried out the new title. "Do you know what this means, Nate?"

Nate laughed. "Let me guess—that you're a lucky boy because you serve the most important man in Virginia."

Chuckling, Sam punched Nate's arm. "Much more than that, Nate. Master Smith comes from a middling sort of family. No better than yours or mine. If he can become the president of Jamestown, then someday you or I could be president. Back in England, we could never dream of such a thing. But here there's no limit to what our future may hold!"

~

On the twenty-ninth of September 1608, Captain Newport arrived in Virginia again. He brought a second supply of provisions and seventy passengers, including two women. Sam watched the women come ashore with an ache in his chest. These were the first English women he'd seen in almost two years. In their long dresses and white caps, either one could have been Sam's mother.

The arrival of the two women stirred up memories of home, but it also boosted everyone's confidence.

"The Virginia Company must be pretty pleased about what we've done over here," one man said. "Else they wouldn't be sending women over. Yes, indeed, we've got us a permanent settlement. Over in England, they must be saying that a man can make himself a living in Virginia! Even have a family."

Along with the two women, the seventy passengers included several craftsmen from Poland and Germany who had been hired by the Virginia Company to develop industries in the colony. Some were skilled glass makers. Sam and Nate were assigned the task of chopping wood for the glass makers' furnace.

"I think I might like to apprentice to a craftsman," Nate told Sam. "Glass making is a skill a man could use anywhere—here or in England. And I like the idea of taking a common thing like sand and making something beautiful and useful out of it."

Sam smiled at his friend. Learning a craft like making glass held no attraction for him. Sam wanted to be outdoors—in the woods or on the boat. He liked exploring new places, like John Smith. He also thought he'd like to farm, like his father. *Someday, the company may let us own farms here. There's so much land in Virginia.*

The mornings had already turned frosty, and gradually the crisp fall weather gave way to cold. At the start of the winter of 1608–1609, Captain Newport sailed back to England. When Sam added up the newcomers from the second supply ship, the passengers from the first supply ships, and those who had survived from the original fleet, he counted over two hundred people now living in the fort. No longer was their colony a small outpost. It had become a town—Jamestown.

Man of the
New World

Now that John Smith was president, he was usually busy with meetings and other matters, so Sam spent less time at his side. Instead, Sam worked with Nate and the new boys from the supply ships on chores around Jamestown. Whenever he could, Sam avoided the adult colonists. So many of these men resented his master! They complained angrily in the boy's presence, and that made Sam uneasy. In particular, the gentlemen hated the way President Smith forced them to do the same work as common laborers.

As president, John Smith had decided there were far too many people living in the fort. "We can't have two hundred people hunting the same ground and fishing the same water," Smith said. "Not during winter, anyway. We'd all starve."

Smith sent groups of settlers to live at outposts along the river. Those settlers who were assigned to move were scared. They didn't want to live away from the security of the fort, so they begged Smith to let them stay. But Smith insisted.

Trade for the Indians' food became more and more difficult. In the last week of December, Smith led a large expedition to Werowocomoco, to meet with Powhatan and discuss the problem. The boats traveled down the James River to the Indian village of Warraskoyack, where the Englishmen camped overnight.

Smith met with Sasenticum, the village chief, who agreed to trade enough food to stock the English boats for the expedition.

In the morning, Sasenticum warned Smith against going to Powhatan's town. He said the emperor planned to betray the Englishmen and seize their guns.

Smith thanked the chief for his warning. "But I have no choice," he explained. "We depend on trade with Powhatan's villages to supply our colony with food. I'm not afraid of Powhatan. I won't hide inside our fort all winter and let him starve us to death. Not while I have guns and ammunition!"

As the Englishmen walked toward the riverbank, Smith called Sam aside. "I told Chief Sasenticum that I wanted to leave a lad here at Warraskoyack," Smith told Sam. "I've spoken to you about the importance of learning the natives' speech and customs. I want you to stay here while I lead the rest of the party to Werowocomoco. Do you understand?"

Sam's heart began to pound, and his eyes darted wildly around the village. *The Warraskoyack villagers seem friendly enough. But I will be all alone here. What if something goes wrong?* Sam tried to blot out the memory that flashed into his mind, the image of George Cassen being tortured in Apokant.

"Sam, I'm speaking to you! Look at me!"

Sam met John Smith's eyes.

"Look, lad," Smith continued. "I already told the chief that I would leave my personal servant here. He agreed to send you back to the fort in a few weeks. That should give you enough time to learn some of the Indians' language. I want you to watch how the villagers hunt, trap, and fish during the winter. I know I can depend on you, Sam. This will be a good test of your resourcefulness."

As soon as Smith said the word, "test," Sam nodded. *Master Smith is right. I can't stay by his side forever.* "I'll gather my gear," he said.

"Sam, tell him you don't want to stay here alone. It's not safe!" Nate hissed as soon as they were out of earshot.

"But I do want to stay, Nate. If I'm going to be a man of Virginia, I need to study the Indians. I'll be safe. Maybe safer than you'll be at Powhatan's village." Sam looked at Nate and declared, "I'm not afraid!" But in his heart Sam knew he really was.

As soon as the English boats disappeared from sight, one of the village women led Sam to her house and showed him where to put down his things. Then she motioned for him to follow her outdoors. Several women were sitting around a fire, twisting hemp between their hands to make strong cord. One woman was kneeling on a piece of hide and scraping off the fur with a shell.

The woman who had taken charge of Sam gently pushed him until he sat down. She dipped a turtle shell into the pot that hung over the fire and offered Sam a taste of stew. It was boiling hot, and Sam blew on it several times before he took a bite. The woman smiled and motioned for Sam to take more.

After he ate, she led Sam to a group of boys. He spent the day tramping through the woods with them. Using hand gestures and words, the boys taught Sam how to set out snares to trap small animals and how to catch fish by hanging a net in the river between stones.

In the days that followed, Sam forgot about his fear of living with these strangers. All of the villagers—men and women—were kind and patient with him. They gladly showed him whatever they were doing and answered his questions. Nobody seemed rushed or discontent. And Sam never heard the villagers shout or argue with each other.

Among the Warraskoyacks, men were hunters. Some of the older boys accompanied the men on hunts, but Sam knew he wouldn't be able to keep up. The men ran long distances through the underbrush in search of game and even longer distances in pursuit of any game they had wounded. Instead, Sam helped the village boys with their work. He spent hours learning to shoot with a bow and arrows. He practiced setting snares and catching fish. The boys taught him dozens of words and howled with laughter when he used the wrong one.

Sam slept in the Indian woman's lodge with her family. At night, with the flaps closed and the fire burning, the lodge was warm and smoky. Everybody slept on benches covered with reed mats. Sam was allowed to cover up with as many soft deerskins as he wanted. The woman even rolled a hide into a long pillow for his head.

Before dawn each morning, all the villagers dipped themselves in the river. Sam wasn't used to bathing every day. At first he refused to take off his clothes and step into the freezing water. But the children giggled, and the woman who had taken charge of him frowned. So on his third morning, Sam peeled off his clothes and forced himself to dash into the icy river. All the village girls smiled when he ran out, his arms and legs covered with goosebumps and his teeth chattering.

In the evenings, the villagers usually danced around the fire between their houses until they felt sleepy. Sam learned to sing their songs, and the boys showed him their dances. After a few days in the village, Sam hardly noticed the Indians' lack of clothing. In fact, the boys persuaded him to leave off his shirt and coat one day and spread bear fat over his chest and arms, as they did. Sam found this protected him from the cold at midday, when he was active, but when the sun went down, he was eager to get back into his coat.

Sam lost track of how many days he lived in Warraskoyack. One morning, the chief called him. Using both words and gestures, he said that three braves would take Sam back to Jamestown. He explained that Sam must not remain any longer because the weather was getting colder. Soon the river would freeze over, making canoe travel impossible.

"Thank you, Chief Sasenticum," Sam said. He tried to use both Indian and English words to make a short speech. "You are a kind *werowance,* and I no longer feel like a stranger, a *tasantasses.* I have lived in your *yihakans*—your houses—and learned many things. Your people are now *wingapoh,* my friends, and I will miss all of you." Sam meant what he said. The Warraskoyacks had treated him as an honored guest and taught him so much.

Chief Sasenticum nodded, a gentle smile on his face. He motioned to one of his men, who handed Sam a cape of animal skins. "*Mescote,*" the chief said.

Sam grinned and wrapped the cape around his shoulders. "Thank you," Sam said. "This *mescote* will keep me warm and help me to remember the Warraskoyacks."

Back at Jamestown, Sam described his stay in Warraskoyack to anybody who would listen. As the food supply in the fort dwindled during the long winter, Sam sometimes wished he could return to the Indian village, where there was always a pot of stew simmering over the fire.

Chief Sasenticum was right—the winter of 1608–09 was extremely cold. Trying to keep warm around their fires, the settlers grumbled and complained about the harsh conditions. John Smith was strict, and he continued to insist that every colonist work, including the highborn gentlemen. He had a simple rule: No work, no food. The punishment for shirking work was exile from the colony. Smith allowed only one exception—sick people, who were fed and cared for until they were strong enough to work again.

During the winter, all the council members died, some from sickness and some from accidents, and John Smith became Jamestown's entire government. His word was the law. Complaints, rumors, and even plots to overthrow Smith multiplied as his authority grew and food became more scarce. In response to every problem, President Smith became more and more forceful.

Jamestown ran dangerously low on food by late winter, and again the Indians refused to trade. Smith lost patience with the chiefs who would not cooperate. He forced them to trade by threatening to destroy their homes and kill their villagers.

Even Sam was nervous about his master's harsh treatment of the Indians. *If we push the Indians any harder, they'll attack us,* Sam worried. He remembered the strength and stamina of the Warraskoyack men. *It's true that we have guns. But the Indians outnumber us by thousands!* He didn't mention his concerns to Smith, though. All the complaints and plots had made John Smith as snappy as a fox in a trap. He would snarl at anybody who so much as offered a suggestion.

By the time the long winter finally began to thaw, the colonists were sharply divided in their opinion of President John Smith. Some believed he had saved them from starvation. Others hated him for treating gentlemen like common laborers or for forcing settlers to live at outposts.

Sam defended his master when the boys complained about him. "John Smith is tough because he has to be. The only way he could keep us from starving was to be tough. Think of Jamestown as a test," Sam said, repeating Smith's words. "Only the strongest and smartest will survive."

In August of 1609, the third supply arrived, the largest supply England had ever sent. Nine ships carrying five hundred settlers—men, women, and children—had set out from England. But the fleet had been battered by hurricanes during the crossing. When the ships straggled up the James River, they were severely damaged. Two of the nine ships, including the one commanded by Captain Newport, did not arrive with the others. On one of the lost ships was the man whom the Virginia Company had appointed to be Jamestown's first governor. He was supposed to replace Smith as the colony's leader.

With this flood of new colonists, Jamestown nearly burst at its seams. Although his term had expired, John Smith remained in charge until the governor arrived.

To house all the newcomers, Smith established two outposts along the James River and sent one hundred and twenty settlers to live at each. One, under the command of Captain Martin, was located downriver, near the mouth of the James, at Nansemond. The other, under the command of Francis West, was located upriver near the falls. That spot was so beautiful that the English named it Nonesuch because there was "none such" a lovely place.

$\sim$

"Sam, make haste!" Smith shouted. He pulled his jack off the peg on the wall.

Sam came running. He held open his master's armored jacket while Smith slid his arms through the sleeves.

"I'm worried about the situation at Nonesuch," Smith said. "I keep getting reports about Indian attacks. Get your armor Sam. We're going up the river to Nonesuch to see for ourselves. I've already ordered the men to get one of the boats ready."

"Why do the Indians keep attacking Nonesuch?" Sam asked.

Smith frowned. There had been repeated Indian attacks at Nonesuch where Francis West was in charge. "Because Francis West is a fool! I've told him over and over that you cannot govern by pleading and coaxing. A commander must command. Indians can spot a weak leader a mile away." Smith stormed out of the house and headed for the river.

When they arrived at Nonesuch, Sam was amazed to find the colonists huddled behind the walls of their small fort, afraid for their lives. John Smith was furious. He sent for Master West and demanded an explanation.

West blamed Smith for failing to send a sufficient supply of gunpowder to the outpost.

"The problem is not the shortage of gunpowder," Smith countered. "I've had reports that you've let the gentlemen here bully and mistreat the nearby villagers. What's needed is strong leadership, Francis. You'll find that if your men don't provoke the Indians, they'll be peaceable enough."

"Watch your tongue, Smith!" West hissed. "Remember who you are speaking to. Since when does a man of your rank feel qualified to instruct me on the duties of leadership?"

Sam's eyes grew round with alarm when he saw John Smith clench his fists. But Smith did not punch West. Instead, he stomped into the fort, identified several of the Nonesuch gentlemen who were causing the problem, and ordered them out of the settlement. He shouted at the other settlers to return to work.

"I'll send gunpowder when we reach Jamestown," Smith told West, his tone icy. "We'll be in more danger aboard the boat than you are here."

After several hours of sailing, Smith ordered the sailors to drop anchor. As they made camp, three men from Nonesuch ran out of the woods, their faces wild with fear. They reported that Indians had attacked as soon as Smith's ship had sailed out of sight. Any settlers working in the fields or woods had been killed.

Smith ordered the boat to return to Nonesuch. As soon as he reached the settlement, he sent some of his men to search for the war party that had attacked the settlement. In spite of West's protests, Smith insisted on putting the settlers back to work.

In a few hours, the culprits were caught: Twelve reckless warriors had attacked the settlement, using surprise and noise to confuse the Englishmen and make them think they were under assault by a large force.

"Why didn't you open fire on them?" Smith asked West. "As soon as they began to run, you would have seen that only a handful of Indians were causing the problem. You could have captured them before they had a chance to ambush the settlers in the fields."

Francis West glared at John Smith. "I blame you for this tragedy, Smith!" snapped West. "When you arrived at my settlement, I reported our shortage of gunpowder. You could have handed over the gunpowder on your boat. But you insisted on making us wait until you returned to Jamestown and sent a supply barge up the river. We were so short of gunpowder that I judged it best to hold our fire until we had a clear view of our attackers."

Sam watched his master's face. Smith's lip quivered and his nostrils flared. "You are in command of one hundred and twenty men at Nonesuch, but you are telling me it's my fault you could not defend yourself against twelve Indians?" Smith yelled. " God help you, Francis West. You've managed to show the savages that Nonesuch is full of frightened mice. Now they're going to snatch you by your tails and roast you for dinner!"

West stared at Smith, his face as pale as parchment. Sam winced. He knew Master Francis West was a very high-ranking gentleman. *No good can come of this,* Sam thought. *Scores of English gentry have come here aboard the ships of the third supply. Surely they will punish John Smith for speaking so harshly to one of their own!*

Smith marched out of Nonesuch Fort. Avoiding West's eyes, Sam followed his master. As soon as they reached the boat, Smith ordered the sailors to haul in the anchor and set the sails. Without another word, he went below deck. When they anchored for the night, their boat was halfway down the river to Jamestown.

In the morning, Smith sent a party of hunters ashore. He ordered the rest of the men to cast out lines for fish. Smith said they would sleep on board again that night and return to Jamestown with their catch the next morning.

It was a fine, cold December night, not a cloud in the sky. The moon was so bright Sam could make out the grain of the ship's planks as he and Nate sat talking on deck. The boys spread out their blankets under the open sky to enjoy the crisp air. John Smith had stretched out on his blanket near the bow of the ship. When the boys finally curled up to sleep, only the footsteps of the night guard disturbed the peaceful rhythm of water lapping at the hull.

Past midnight, the boys were awakened by a loud *bang* followed by a man's scream. Sam sprang to his feet, peering through the darkness.

"What's wrong?" Nate hissed as he got up and stood beside Sam.

"I'm on fire!" howled John Smith.

Before Sam could locate his master, Smith tore past the boys. The bottom of his shirt was in flames. Smith vaulted over the ship's rail and plunged into the river. Sam grabbed the rail and watched as Smith hit the water. Sam glanced at Nate, and without a word, both boys ripped off their shirts and jumped into the river after Smith.

The cold of the water sliced through Sam's body. He bobbed to the surface, his teeth chattering, and searched for Smith. When his master came up, gasping for air, both boys streaked toward him. But before they could reach him, he went under again. Sam dove, grabbed at something moving in the black waters, but found he was holding Nate's hair as both boys popped back to the surface. "There!" Nate shouted. "He's over there!"

Sam wheeled around and saw a glistening black hump floating on the water. Both boys struggled toward it and groped for John Smith. Holding him by his hair and arms, they pulled his limp body to the side of the ship. With the help of a rope thrown out by the sailors, Smith was hauled aboard.

Smith vaulted over the rail and plunged into the river.

As soon as Sam climbed onto the deck, he ran to the dark figure dripping on the boards. Smith moaned, and Sam closed his eyes and said a short prayer of thanks that his master was alive. Then he fell to his knees, exhausted, and watched the men peel off Smith's wet, charred shirt. Sam winced at the sight. Smith's thigh had been badly burned. In the center of the wound, the flesh was bright red, streaked with black. To Sam it looked like a large, ripe strawberry that had been torn open by a bird's beak and splashed with mud. Bubbly blisters trailed away from the raw wound across Smith's stomach and leg.

Sam felt Nate's hand touch his shoulder. The boys were dripping wet, shivering in the cold night air. Nate got up and grabbed two blankets. He draped one around Sam's shoulders and wrapped the other around himself.

Sam watched the men dry his master. At every touch, Smith gritted his teeth. His mouth opened to scream, but with a mighty effort he stifled the sound before it formed.

When the men laid Smith on a dry blanket, he spoke at last. "How did this happen? How did my shirt catch fire while I was sleeping?"

After a pause, the night guard answered, his voice small and frightened. "It was an accident, Cap'n. I swear it was! I heard something splashing in the river, and I turned to see what was going on. I didn't doze off—only turned to look, that's all." The man's words tumbled out breathlessly. "It happened so fast. I didn't know my powder was on fire."

"Explain yourself, man," asked one of the others, "You turned to look at something in the river. How did that set your powder can on fire?"

"When I turned, my m-match caught the edge of my collar on fire," the guard stammered. "So I ripped off my powder can and tossed it away. I had to get rid of it, didn't I? Else it would catch fire and blow up." He locked eyes with the men. "I swear I didn't realize the can was burning when I tossed it away."

"You tossed your flaming powder can at the Cap'n?"

"I didn't mean to throw it at him!" he cried. "I just tore it off my neck and tossed it aside so I could slap out the fire on my collar. Next thing I knew, there was a *bang.*" The night guard's voice began to tremble. "It wasn't my fault, don't you see? Cap'n Smith has a lot of enemies, but I was never in favor of killing him."

"Killing him!" screamed Sam. He jumped to his feet. "He's going to die?"

One of the men put his hands on Sam's shoulders, but he avoided the boy's eyes. "Nobody meant that Cap'n's going to die, Sam. The guard's just rambling because he's upset. We'll set sail for Jamestown as soon as the sky lightens. The surgeons will look at your master. John Smith is as strong a man as I've ever met, that's sure. And he's had many a brush with death and lived to tell his story."

The men urged Sam to get some rest, but he sat by his master's side as the boat sailed down the river. Sam wasn't convinced that the gunpowder explosion was an accident. *Even as the guard told his story,* Sam remembered, *the man admitted he knew of plots to kill John Smith.* Until Smith was well enough to defend himself, Sam decided he would have to be his master's eyes, ears, and hands.

The boat dropped anchor at Jamestown the next afternoon, and Sam helped the men carry his wounded master up to the fort on a blanket. Smith was in a great deal of pain. His face was white, and he clenched his teeth to keep from screaming. The surgeons spread salve on the wound and covered it with dressings, then bled Smith to cleanse his body of infection. Sam stayed nearby, ready to run for any supplies that might be needed.

That night, Sam and Nate took turns watching beside Smith. Their patient tossed and turned in misery. Smith could not stand the touch of a blanket against his wound. The boys built up the fire in the room so he wouldn't become chilled.

For the next few days, Smith could barely hobble. Every movement made him grimace, and the mere flap of his shirt against his wound was agonizing. On the fourth day after his accident, Smith awoke in a terrible sweat. Sam ran to the river to fill a pitcher with cool water, and he soaked rags to lay on his master's forehead. Nate went to get the surgeons, but both boys knew what Smith's fever meant: His wound had become infected!

During the long days and nights that followed, Sam's master slept fitfully, waking with a high fever that sometimes made him delirious. At times, Smith shot out of bed, ranting and screaming. It took both boys to hold him down. When he slept again, his head thrashed from side to side, and he moaned pitifully.

Although Sam had never treated a burn before, he knew Smith was not healing. The raw skin oozed and festered, soaking through bandages. One day, Sam asked the surgeon if his master would survive. The man frowned as he met Sam's eye. Instead of answering, he shrugged.

The sailors had already begun packing the supply ships with Virginia goods to sell in England. The colony's gentlemen decided to send John Smith back on these ships. If he survived the crossing, skilled doctors in London could care for him. Smith was too weak to protest.

He called the boys to his side. "You've done very well in Jamestown, Nathaniel Peacock," Smith said, with his eyes closed and a weak smile on his face. "Stephen Calthrop would be proud of the young man you've become. He shared my belief in Virginia, you know."

Sam looked at Nate. *My master is talking like a man who expects to die,* he thought with an ache in his chest.

"A new world this will be," Smith continued, "for smart, ambitious men. That's what Stephen and I used to say. A place where strong fellows will succeed. No matter about the gold or the passage to the Orient. There are enough riches in this land without the sparkle of gold or the touch of silk. You'll enjoy a prosperous future here, Nate."

"Master Smith, please," Nate said, "Let me return to England with you and Sam. I have no love for this land. Ever since Master Calthrop died...."

Smith put his finger on his lips. "I know how hard Stephen's death was for you, Nate. But there comes a time when a boy takes his place as a man. Time to leave the past behind. Stephen Calthrop wanted this future for you."

"If it's a man I'm to be from now on, then it's for me to decide my own future," Nate said. "Please Master Smith, I want to return to England."

Smith opened his eyes. "I'm not going to force you to stay here, Nate. You've earned the right to choose your future. But don't make your decision lightly. Be sure that returning to England is what you want."

"I'm sure, Master Smith," Nate said firmly.

"And you, Samuel Collier?" Smith asked gently. "Nate can care for me on the voyage to England, so I won't be requiring your services any longer. What will you choose?"

Sam looked at Nate. Ever since the boys had set sail from England on this great adventure, Nate had been his companion. He was the best friend Sam had ever known, closer to him than his brother. Sam hesitated. He thought about his family's farm in Lincolnshire, and he could picture Thomas at work in the barn. He remembered his mother's soft eyes and how her cheeks wrinkled when she smiled. Oh, how he longed to see her again! Sam could almost feel the reassuring warmth of his father's hand on his shoulder as he greeted his younger son. How good it would be to see his home and his family again!

John Smith and Nate both watched him. Sam gazed at Smith, the man's pale face lined with days of suffering. Sam thought about how much he owed this forceful man. Smith had led him out of the small, narrow world of his childhood and shown him so many things—wonderful, strange, and threatening things— things he could never have imagined.

"Sam, this colony will need men like you, men with brains and courage," Smith said slowly. "There's no need for both you and Nate to return to England just to care for me aboard the ship. This will likely be my last crossing, anyway." Smith reached for Sam's hand. "You're as near to a son as I will ever have, Samuel Collier, and Jamestown is the greatest achievement of my life. But the future belongs to you. What will you choose?"

Sam hesitated. "I thought I was the luckiest boy in England to sail across the ocean and explore Virginia," he said. "Even when life in Jamestown was the most terrible, I was sure that I was destined to become a man in this new world. If my service to you is over, Master Smith, then that's what I choose." He looked at Nate, then at Smith. "I'll stay here in Virginia."

Sam and Nate packed Smith's belongings and helped the sailors carry him aboard the ship. When all was ready, and the ship was about to sail, Sam clasped John Smith's hands. He wanted to thank him, to tell him how much he had learned from him. But he didn't know how to explain what he was feeling. Instead, he said, "I won't forget you. Whenever I think about coming to Virginia to plant this colony, I'll remember John Smith."

Then he turned to Nate and put his hands on his friend's shoulders. "Godspeed, Nathaniel Peacock. I don't know when our paths will cross again." Sam's throat tightened and his cheeks felt hot. Holding back tears, he punched Nate's shoulder.

Nate reached up, pulled Sam's cap off his head, and flung it. The boys watched the cap sail over the ship's rail, clear the bank, and land on dry ground. Nate laughed. "Always the lucky fellow! I won't be worrying about you. Farewell, Samuel Collier of Virginia!"

This novel is based on the history of Jamestown, the first permanent English settlement in North America. All of the character's names and major events are true. But many of the details about the lives of the early settlers are not known, so I've speculated about what might have happened. I made up conversations and personalities to create a story. This book is based on primary sources—accounts and letters written by John Smith and other settlers—but it is historical fiction.

How much is true about Sam Collier and the other boys? What happened to them?

Four boys were listed on the first fleet of ships that traveled to Virginia. According to the settlers' accounts, one boy was killed during the 1607 assault by Indians on the fort, but that boy's identity is unknown.

Of the four boys, historians know the most about Samuel Collier. This boy was mentioned as Smith's page after the settlers arrived in Virginia. Collier accompanied Smith on at least two expeditions into Indian villages. On the expedition to Powhatan's town in 1608–09, he was left in the Indian village of Warraskoyack to learn the natives' language and customs. Collier did remain in Virginia after Smith's return to England in 1609.

Collier survived the colony's most difficult time, which was the winter of 1609–10, and he lived for another twelve years in Jamestown. During the winter of 1622–23, he was accidentally shot and killed by an English guard. John Smith mentioned Collier's death in his 1624 book, *The General History of Virginia, New-England, & the Summer Isles.* He wrote, "Samuell Collyer one of the most ancientest Planters, and very well acquainted with their [the Indian's] language and habitation, humors and conditions, and Governor of a Towne, when the Watch was set going the round, unfortunately by a Centinell that discharged his peece, was slaine."

Historians know very little about the background, and nothing about the physical characteristics and personalities of these four boys. Although I used real names for my characters, all the descriptions of them are made up. As more information is discovered, we may learn that one or another of these boys was brave or clever, strong or kind. Until that time, we can only guess how they responded to the difficult conditions they faced in Jamestown.

Did John Smith survive his injury? What happened to him?

Yes, Smith survived the gunpowder accident. After his return to England, he wrote and published books about his Jamestown experiences. John Smith's map of the Chesapeake and points north was so accurate that it was used as the basis for maps of the area for more than a hundred years.

In 1614, he returned to North America and explored Massachusetts Bay. He gave this area the name, "New England."

John Smith died in 1631, at about 51 years of age. He never married, and he never returned to Jamestown.

Why isn't Pocahontas a major character in this book?

Although the story describing how Pocahontas saved John Smith's life has captured the popular imagination, it may not have happened at all! Smith did not mention this incident until years after he left Virginia. Some historians think that he may have made it up to attract some of the attention that his countrymen were giving to Pocahontas, who was visiting England as the wife of John Rolfe.

What happened in Jamestown after John Smith returned to England?

The most terrible period in Jamestown's history, the "starving time," happened right after Smith's departure, during the winter of 1609–10. Of the roughly three hundred and fifty people living in the colony at the start of that winter, only ninety survived!

One of the lost ships of the third supply, the *Sea Venture*—commanded by Captain Newport and carrying Sir Thomas Gates, the governor appointed by the Virginia Company—shipwrecked in 1609 in Bermuda, where passengers and crew spent the winter. They arrived in Virginia in May of 1610, and they found such gruesome conditions that they decided to abandon the settlement. However, they changed their minds when they learned that a new supply was arriving from England with one hundred and fifty settlers and plenty of provisions. This fourth supply arrived in June. It was commanded by Lord De La Warr, who would take over as Jamestown's governor.

For the next few years, Jamestown was put under martial law and great progress was made in building and planting. The colonists discovered that tobacco was a highly successful cash crop for the region. As more colonists arrived, settlements were established east and west of the original site along the James River.

Jamestown was the center of colonial Virginia for ninety-two years. In 1698, after a major fire, the seat of colonial government was moved to Middle Plantation, which was renamed Williamsburg. Gradually, the site of the original settlement was abandoned.

How do people know what happened during the settlement of Jamestown?

Some of the early settlers wrote accounts of their experiences. These were sent in letters to friends and relatives in England or published in books. John Smith wrote several long narratives about the colony's early years. Other information comes from archaeological investigations, which are still underway.

Where can you learn more about Jamestown?

You can visit the site of the original settlement, which is owned by the Association for the Preservation of Virginia Antiquities (APVA) and the Colonial National Historical Park, part of the National Park Service. Archaeologists are uncovering tools, weapons, skeletal remains, foundations of buildings— all of which provide pieces to the puzzle about what happened during the colony's early years.

Near the site is a living history museum called Jamestown Settlement, which is run by the state of Virginia. Costumed interpreters help visitors discover the daily lives of the original settlers, as well as their Native American neighbors. Replicas of the first fleet of ships to reach Jamestown are docked on the river beside the re-created settlement, and visitors are welcome on board. A building contains displays and artifacts.

You can visit the APVA's website at www.apva.org, the Colonial National Historical Park's website at www.nps.gov/colo, and Jamestown Settlement's website at www.historyisfun.org.

About the Author

GAIL LANGER KARWOSKI, a former teacher of elementary, middle, and high school students, frequently returns to schools as a visiting author. She also wrote QUAKE! DISASTER IN SAN FRANCISCO, 1906, SEAMAN: THE DOG WHO EXPLORED THE WEST WITH LEWIS AND CLARK, and cowrote THE TREE THAT OWNS ITSELF AND OTHER STORIES FROM OUT OF GEORGIA'S PAST with Loretta Hammer. Karwoski received her B.A. from the University of Massachusetts and her M.A. from the University of Minnesota, later earning her elementary and gifted teaching certificates at the University of Georgia. She lives with her family in Oconee County, Georgia.

About the Illustrator

PAUL CASALE, a native of Brooklyn, New York, received his B.F.A from the Pratt Institute. A member of the prestigious Society of Illustrators in New York City, Casale has illustrated many children's books. He lives with his family in New Jersey.